"All right, Dez. How much is it worth for me to get into a hot tub with you?"

The woman *was* trying to kill him, Dez decided. She hadn't managed to choke him to death with coffee, so she'd opted to try stopping his heart with astonishment.

"How much is it worth to you?" Gina repeated. "Because for—say—ten thousand dollars, I'd consider it."

"Ten *thousand*—" He cleared his throat and tried again. "You have an inflated idea of what an evening of your time is worth."

He could almost hear ice cubes tinkling in her voice. "And let's make it quite clear that my time is absolutely all I'm talking about."

"No hanky-panky in the hot tub," he agreed smoothly.

WHAT WOMEN WANT!

It could happen to you...

Every woman has dreams—deep desires, all-consuming passions, or maybe just little everyday wishes! In this brand-new miniseries from Tender Romance® we're delighted to present a series of fresh, lively and compelling stories by some of our most popular authors—all exploring the truth about what women *really* want.

Step into each heroine's shoes as we get up close and personal with her most cherished dreams...big *and* small!

- Is she a high-flying executive...but all she wants is a baby?
- Has she met her ideal man—if only he wasn't her new boss...
- Is she about to marry, but is secretly in love with someone else?
- Or does she simply long to be slimmer, more glamorous, with a whole new wardrobe!

Whatever she wants, each heroine finds happiness on her own terms—and unexpected romance along the way. And she's about to discover whether Mr. Right is the answer to her dreams—or if he has a few questions of his own!

Look out for the next book in this exciting new miniseries!

The Forbidden Marriage
by Rebecca Winters (#3768)
On sale October

THE BILLIONAIRE BID
Leigh Michaels

WHAT WOMEN WANT!
It could happen to you...

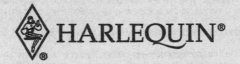

HARLEQUIN®

TORONTO • NEW YORK • LONDON
AMSTERDAM • PARIS • SYDNEY • HAMBURG
STOCKHOLM • ATHENS • TOKYO • MILAN • MADRID
PRAGUE • WARSAW • BUDAPEST • AUCKLAND

ISBN 0-373-03759-7

THE BILLIONAIRE BID

First North American Publication 2003.

Visit us at www.eHarlequin.com

Printed in U.S.A.

CHAPTER ONE

WHEN Gina reached the restaurant, she was relieved to see that she was a few minutes early. Not only would it be bad manners to keep a guest waiting, but in this case it would be purely stupid. She had one shot at this presentation. If she couldn't pull it off today, the plan wouldn't fly at all. So she'd take advantage of the extra few minutes to go over her mental notes once more.

The maître d' looked her over doubtfully. "Would you like to wait in the bar, Ms. Haskell? Or at your table?"

"The table, I believe. My companion will be arriving within a few minutes. You do know Mrs. Garrett, don't you? Anne Garrett?"

The man's expression didn't so much as flicker, but his voice was cool. "Certainly I know the publisher of the local newspaper, Ms. Haskell." He didn't show her to the table; he snapped his fingers and a subordinate arrived to escort her instead.

Dumb question, Gina thought philosophically. If she'd tried, she couldn't have made it clearer that she was moving outside her normal circles. *Next time, why don't you just ask him if the fish is fresh? He couldn't be any more insulted by that.*

If there ever was a next time, of course. There weren't many occasions for Gina to go to a really first-class restaurant.

In fact, though she'd lived in Lakemont much of her life, Gina had never been inside The Maple Tree before. As the waiter seated her, she took a quick—and, she hoped, un-

5

obtrusive—glance at her surroundings. The dining room was large, but because the tables were set far apart there weren't as many of them as she would have expected. Though she could hear the murmur of voices from the ones nearest to hers, she couldn't have eavesdropped even if she'd tried. Not only the distance between tables but the soft tinkle of ragtime music in the background prevented it.

The decorating scheme seemed to have been adopted from the restaurant's name; as if to make the point, on one wall was a grouping of arty photographs of trees and individual leaves. The walls and carpet were the soft green of new leaves, while the table linens were a splash of autumn colors—red napkins against pale gold tablecloths. Unusual though it was, Gina thought the effect was stunning.

At the far end of the room sat a glossy grand piano next to a small dance floor, and along one side of the dining room was a bar. Its wood surface—no doubt it was maple to fit the theme, Gina thought—was so highly polished that it gleamed nearly as brightly as the brass that accented it.

For an upscale restaurant at lunchtime, she thought, the bar seemed strangely quiet. In fact, there was only one man sitting there, occupying the tall stool at the end nearest to Gina's table. He thumped his index finger against his glass, and the bartender moved toward him and picked up the glass. The man turned toward the room and with no warning whatsoever looked directly into Gina's eyes.

She felt herself turning pink. It was one of the hazards of being a redhead—though in this case it was perfectly ridiculous to feel the slightest embarrassment. It wasn't as if she'd been watching him—it was pure coincidence that she had happened to be facing his direction when he'd turned.

No matter what he might think, he hadn't caught her doing anything rude—which was more than she could say for him at the moment. A gentleman would have made momentary eye contact and then looked away. But this man...

He tipped his head back a fraction of an inch. His eyes narrowed. He settled an elbow on the bar as if to brace himself while he looked her over to his satisfaction.

Gina felt like walking over to him and making it absolutely clear that she hadn't been staring at him—or indeed at anything. But to do that would only call more attention to an episode which had already gotten far bigger than it had any reason to. She'd merely been looking around the room, appreciating the ambience and the decor. It certainly wasn't her fault he'd happened to be in the way, blocking her view.

She opened the menu the waiter had left. But the words inside looked strangely blurry, as if once she'd focused her gaze on the man at the bar she couldn't get her eyes to adjust to a different distance. She unfolded her napkin and fussed with laying it out just right on her lap. She reminded herself that these last few minutes of quiet would be better used to review the presentation she would be making over lunch.

None of it worked. Her senses were still on high alert, because he was still watching her. Even without looking up, she knew it.

Fine, Gina told herself irritably. *Two can play that game. What's good for the goose...*

She pushed the menu aside. This time she didn't bother with a survey of the room; he'd only interpret that as coyness anyway. She put both elbows on the edge of the table, rested her chin on her fingertips, and stared back at him.

Actually, she had to admit, he wasn't a bad addition to

either the ambience or the decor. He was tall; she could tell that much from the way he was half sitting on the high stool with one foot hooked easily onto the rung and the other still planted on the floor. And he was good-looking in a hard-edged fashion, with blue-black hair, a strong jaw, and a proud nose. Of course, she'd never been much interested in the dark, predatory type.

What, she wondered, had made him bore in on her? Surely he didn't stare at every woman who glanced at him as Gina had done—or even every woman who took a long hard second look. For one thing, if he did he'd have no time left to do anything else, because there must be plenty of women who—unlike Gina—would find that package attractive enough to inspect at length.

Without taking his gaze off Gina, the man at the bar stretched out a hand unerringly for his replenished glass and held it up, as if offering a toast to her.

Well, Haskell, that didn't exactly turn out the way you planned. Now what?

The man shifted on the bar stool as if he was about to rise. Gina tensed. *If he comes over here...*

Beside her, the maître d' cleared his throat loudly.

Startled, Gina jumped up. Her chair rocked, coming dangerously close to upsetting. Her napkin trailed off her lap onto the floor, and the edge of her suit jacket snagged on the corner of the menu and flipped it off the table. Gina felt color flood her face. The man at the bar, she thought, must be enjoying this show immensely. Fortunately, because of the way the table was angled, he couldn't see her face now. Even better, she couldn't see him anymore.

The maître d', looking as if he were suffering from a sudden cramp, waved a busboy over to retrieve the menu and bring a fresh napkin while he pulled out a chair for her guest. "Mrs. Garrett," he said, enunciating very carefully.

As if he felt it necessary to introduce us, Gina thought irritably.

Anne Garrett stretched a hand across the table. "Hello, Gina. It's nice to see you again." She glanced up at the maître d' and added dryly, "Thank you, Bruce. I believe I can handle it from here."

The maître d' looked skeptical, but he retreated.

"Sorry," Gina said, feeling breathless. "I'm not usually quite so clumsy." *I will not look at the bar,* she told herself. Seeing amusement in those deep-set eyes would not help matters.

I wonder what color his eyes are, anyway.

"Bruce's evil stare would make Saint Peter feel guilty," Anne murmured. "I've always wondered how many of the waiters he hires last a full week without having a nervous breakdown." She opened her menu. "I'm sorry to say I only have an hour before I have to be back at the newspaper for one of those ghastly endless meetings. So let's order first, if you don't mind, and then you can tell me what's going on."

Gina's throat tightened as time seemed to compress around her. An hour wasn't nearly long enough... Though, on the other hand, if she couldn't convince Anne Garrett of the value of her plan in an hour, then she probably couldn't do it in a week either. And if she couldn't convince Anne Garrett...

What a cheerful thought that is.

Gina ordered a salad almost at random, sipped her iced tea, and began. "First I want to thank you for meeting with me. I appreciate being able to get your advice, since where Lakemont is concerned, you're an expert."

Anne paused with the cream pitcher suspended above her coffee cup. "I wouldn't go quite that far. I'm a native, but so are you—aren't you?"

"Not quite. And I don't have nearly the contacts you do."

Anne set the cream down and picked up her spoon. "So tell me what it is you want from my contacts."

Gina wanted to choke herself. That hadn't been very neatly done at all. "It's the museum," she said, and sighed. "Oh, that sounded foolish, didn't it? Of course it's the museum. You were gracious enough to show an interest in it when you visited a couple of weeks ago."

"Of course I'm interested. It's a nice little museum, full of history."

"And that's the point." Gina ran a hand over the nape of her neck. It felt just a little itchy; the man at the bar must still be watching her. "Lakemont and Kerrigan County deserve more than just a *nice little museum,* one that's so short of space it's crammed full with no place to turn around. Just last week we were offered the stained-glass windows from St. Francis Church. It's probably going to be torn down before long, you know. But we don't have a shed big enough to store the windows in, much less a place to display them."

The waiter returned with their salads. When he was finished arranging the table, Anne drizzled dressing over the crabmeat which topped her salad and said, "So you're asking for a donation for...what? To remodel a room for the windows?"

"Not exactly." Gina took a deep breath and plunged. "That would be a start, but I want to reconstruct the entire museum."

Anne Garrett's eyebrows climbed. "Put up a new building, you mean?"

"No—oh, no." The thought was like a knife to Gina's heart. "A new building for a museum of history? It would be anachronous."

"The house you're in now must be a hundred and fifty years old."

Gina nodded. "And the museum has been there from its beginning. You see, there wouldn't be a museum at all if it hadn't been for Essie Kerrigan. She not only started the Kerrigan County Historical Society, but she kept it going almost single-handed for years. Her possessions formed the nucleus of the collection, her money filled the gaps whenever there was a shortfall in the budget, and her house has provided a roof to shelter it. She devoted her entire life to creating and nurturing it."

"But Essie's gone now, and you're the director. So you can do whatever you think best."

Gina smiled wryly. "I still wouldn't consider a modern building. For one thing, Essie would haunt it—and if she were to be surrounded by wallboard and cheap pine moldings, she would not be a happy ghost. Besides, there's the problem of where to put a new building. A museum of history needs to be in the historical area, not the suburbs—and that means near downtown."

"Near the lakefront, where land is scarce and expensive."

"Exactly."

"So if it's not a new building you want, what do you have in mind? My kids and I had a very pleasant afternoon at the museum, you know—so I'm having trouble seeing what could possibly need to be changed."

"A pleasant afternoon." Gina put down her fork and leaned forward. "I'm glad you enjoyed your visit, but would you come back again? No, don't answer right away—that's a serious question. In a couple of hours you saw everything we have room to display. Unless we can create more space, room for changing exhibits, there's no reason for anyone to visit more than once. And unless we have repeat traffic—regular visitors—then the museum can't possibly support itself. So let me ask again. Would you come back for another visit?''

Anne sighed. ''Probably not anytime soon.''

''That's precisely my point. The museum is now at the stage where it needs to grow, or else it's going to die.'' Gina stabbed a tomato chunk.

''What sort of growth are you talking about?'' Anne Garrett sounded doubtful.

Gina felt herself wavering. Maybe it would be wise to pull back a bit? Sometimes people who asked for the moon ended by getting nothing at all.

No, she thought. It was true, of course, that if she aimed too high, she might miss altogether. But if she aimed too low, she'd always wonder if she could have done better. And it would be the museum that would suffer. Essie Kerrigan's precious museum. Gina couldn't let that happen.

''I want to renovate the entire building,'' she said firmly. ''It's been years since there has been any more than make-do maintenance—for instance, we've patched the roof, but it really needs to be replaced. Then I want to restructure the interior to provide real galleries instead of cramped spaces that will hardly hold a display cabinet.''

''I can't imagine Essie would like seeing you do that to her house.''

''She wouldn't be thrilled,'' Gina admitted. ''But she understood the need. She said herself that it was a shame we couldn't have more wide-open space, and better lighting. And security, of course—you have no idea how difficult it is now to keep an eye on every visitor.''

Anne smiled wryly. ''I thought it was lovely to have a private tour guide showing us around. Eleanor—was that her name? I never considered that she was really a guard, making sure we didn't walk off with anything.''

Gina winced at her own lack of tact. "We don't like to think of our volunteers as guards. But security is a problem, because we never have enough people on hand. I'd also like to build a couple of new wings for additional gallery space."

"Where?" Anne sounded incredulous. "You don't have room to build on wings."

"Well, we don't need a backyard. Or a driveway, for that matter." Gina moved a slice of black olive to the side of her salad. "I want to make it clear, by the way, that I'm not asking you for the money."

"That's a relief," Anne murmured.

"But it's going to take some major fund-raising, and I hoped you might have some ideas."

"And you'd like the support of the newspaper when you start your campaign, I suppose."

Gina admitted, "That, too." If the *Chronicle* were to endorse the idea of a museum expansion, the publicity would make raising the money much easier.

Anne stirred her lettuce with an abstracted air. "And I thought perhaps you'd asked me to lunch merely to invite me to join the board," she mused.

Gina sat still, almost afraid to breathe. Afraid to interrupt.

As the silence drew out, her neck started to feel itchy again. The sensation of being watched had never quite gone away, though she'd tried her best to suppress the feeling so she could concentrate on the museum. She'd caught herself several times running a hand over the nape of her neck, as if to brush away an insect—or a bothersome stare.

She couldn't stand it anymore. She had to look. If he was still sitting there staring at her...

But the stool at the end of the bar was empty. He was gone. Her feeling of being watched must have been merely a shadow, an impression which had lingered on because of the intensity of his gaze.

How foolish, she told herself, to feel just a little let down. She'd wanted him to stop looking and go away. Hadn't she?

She gave up on her unfinished salad—the lettuce seemed to have kept growing even after it was arranged on her plate—and glanced around the room while she waited for Anne to gather her thoughts. Her gaze came to rest on a pair of men at a nearby table.

He hadn't left after all. He'd only moved.

And of course, the instant she spotted him, he turned his head and looked directly at her, as if her gaze had acted like a magnet.

She couldn't stand it an instant longer. Gina said abruptly, "The man at the third table over. In front of the fireplace. Who is he?"

Anne looked puzzled. "There are two men at that table," she pointed out. "Which one are you asking about?"

"The one who looks like an eagle."

"Looks like a *what?*"

"You know," Gina said impatiently. "Proud and stern and looking for prey."

Anne's eyebrows lifted. "Well, that's not a bad description. Especially the part about prey. I thought you'd know him, since he's some kind of cousin or nephew of Essie's. His name's Dez Kerrigan."

Gina knew the name, of course. Essie had been just as devoted to genealogy as to every other sort of history, and so Gina had heard a lot about the various branches of the Kerrigans. But she'd never met him; he obviously hadn't been as interested in the family as Essie had been, or he'd have come 'round once in a while to visit his aunt or cousin or whatever Essie was to him.

And there was something else she should remember about him—something Essie had said. The memory nagged at the back of Gina's brain, but it wouldn't come out in the open. She clearly remembered Essie making the comment, because it had verged on sounding catty, and that wasn't like Essie. But she couldn't remember for the life of her what Essie had said.

"Now *that's* interesting," Anne murmured. "Why do you want to know?"

Sanity returned just in time. *You're an idiot,* Gina thought, *to call attention to yourself like that. Making a journalist wonder why you're fascinated by a particular man...*

"Just wondering." Gina tried to keep her voice casual. "And what's so interesting? That Essie's nephew is having lunch here?"

"No. Who he's having lunch with." Anne put her napkin down. "I'm sorry, Gina. I must get back to the office."

Gina put out a hand. "I understand that you may not want to commit yourself in any way just now. But—"

"But you want to hear my instant opinion anyway. All right. For what it's worth, I believe you're thinking on much too small a scale."

"Too *small?*" Gina asked blankly.

Anne nodded. She pulled out a business card and scrawled something on the back of it. "By the way, I'm having a cocktail party Sunday night. You can meet some of your potential donors on neutral territory and size them up before you officially start asking for money. Here's the address. And now I really need to run—but be sure you read the newspaper in the morning."

Before Gina could ask what tomorrow's *Lakemont Chronicle* could possibly have to do with anything, she was gone.

* * *

Gina was habitually an early riser, a habit ingrained from her upbringing. But on the following morning she was awake well before dawn, waiting to hear the distinctive off-key whine of the newspaper carrier's car engine idling down the street while he tossed bundles onto front porches.

She'd never felt anything but safe here, even though the neighborhood, once an exclusive enclave, was now hemmed in on all sides by commercial and industrial development. She'd lived in a lot of places that were worse. Still, she couldn't blame a parent for not allowing a kid on a bike to deliver the morning newspaper.

Which brought her squarely back to the question of what was supposed to be so special about this morning's newspaper. Or was that simply Anne Garrett's way of saying goodbye—taking every opportunity to promote the newspaper she published? Surely not.

Gina made herself a cup of instant coffee and sat down by the window in her living room, which overlooked the front door of the brown-brick row house. Once the building had housed a single family, along with their servants, but years ago it had been split into rental units. Gina's apartment had originally been the family's bedrooms.

She liked being up high, even though hauling everything upstairs got to be a pain after a while. And she liked the feeling of space that the tall ceilings of an old house offered. Besides, her apartment was close to work; the Kerrigan County Historical Museum was only three blocks down the street and around a corner, so Gina didn't need to keep a car. A good thing, too, since there was no place for her to park it except in the museum's driveway—a driveway that, with any luck, would soon disappear under a new gallery.

You're thinking on much too small a scale, Anne Garrett

had told her. Well, that was easy for Anne to say, with the resources of the *Chronicle* behind her.

It was true, Gina admitted, that the long, narrow strip of concrete next to Essie Kerrigan's house was not large enough for the spacious, airy galleries she'd like to have. But if they pushed out the back of the house as well, essentially roofing in the entire garden…

There still wouldn't be room for things like the windows from St. Francis Church, regrettable though the loss would be. But Gina had to work with the raw material she'd been given, as sensitively as it was possible to do.

Of course, they'd leave the front facade just as it had been constructed by Essie's grandfather Desmond Kerrigan—at least as far as they could. It would be criminal to destroy that wide, spacious open porch and corner tower. So long as the addition on the driveway side was stepped back so it didn't overwhelm the front of the building, it would still look all right.

Desmond Kerrigan hadn't been the first of his name to come to Lakemont, and he wasn't the Kerrigan that the county had been named for. But he had been the first of the family to consistently turn small investments into large ones, so when he'd built his home in what was then the most exclusive section of Lakemont, he hadn't pinched pennies. He'd built solid and strong—but even so, a century and a half had taken a toll on the house as well as on the neighborhood. The red brick had long ago been darkened by city smoke and fumes. Hailstorms through the years had left behind cracked and broken roof slates.

In the last years of her life, Essie Kerrigan had not had energy to take care of those things, and so delayed building maintenance was one of the jobs that had fallen to Gina when she'd assumed Essie's title as head of the museum.

And as long as they would have to raise money for restoration, why not go the whole way and expand at the same time?

Essie had understood the need to expand the museum, though she had sighed over the idea of adding modern wings to her beloved old house. Gina wondered what Dez Kerrigan would think of the plan.

Not that he would have any say in what the museum board did, of course. The house had been Essie's, and the will she had written couldn't have made her intentions any clearer. Still, Gina supposed that the other branches of the family might have feelings about the matter. And one who had apparently been named after the distant ancestor who had built the house in the first place might have strong sentiments indeed.

Gina wondered if Dez Kerrigan had known who she was yesterday. Was that why he'd been staring—looking at her not as a woman, but as the person who had—in a manner of speaking—ended up in possession of Desmond Kerrigan's house?

It couldn't be any more than that, she was certain. If he'd known about her plans for expansion, he might well object—even though he had no real right to an opinion. But the fact was he couldn't possibly know about that. The plans were still so tentative that the only people she'd discussed them with were the members of the museum's board and Anne Garrett. They hadn't even hired an architect yet.

On the other hand, Gina thought, his reaction yesterday probably had nothing at all to do with the museum. Her first assessment of Dez Kerrigan had probably been the correct one—the man was simply rude. He thought he'd caught her staring at him, and he'd taken it as license to stare back.

What was it about the man that she ought to remember, but couldn't? She was certain Essie had said something about him. Not that it was important—but if she had time today when she got to work, she'd dig out Essie's family history files. Essie had noted down every jot of information she'd dug out, every source and reference, even her every suspicion. Somewhere in there should be the clue to Dez Kerrigan.

Gina heard three distinct thumps on the front porch—her newspaper, along with those of her upstairs and downstairs neighbors. As quietly as she could, watching out for the creaky stair, Gina went down to retrieve her copy. She spread it carefully on the old trunk which doubled as a coffee table, flipped through the pages once to see if anything leaped out at her, and then refilled her coffee cup and settled down to look at each individual story.

Million-dollar verdict in civil suit—but it was unlikely the winner was the type to donate money to a historical museum. *City councilman challenges mayor*—nothing unusual about that. *Tyler-Royale expected to close downtown store—five hundred jobs at stake—formal announcement expected today…* That kind of blow to the community's economy wouldn't make raising money for a museum expansion any easier.

Gina turned the page, then turned it back and sat staring at the picture of the Tyler-Royale department store building. There were two pictures, in fact—one of a group of clerks beside an old-fashioned cash register, taken when the store was brand new nearly a century before, and a shot from just yesterday of shoppers at the front entrance.

You're thinking too small, Anne Garrett had said. And then *Be sure you read the newspaper.*

Had she…could she have been…thinking about the Tyler-Royale building as a home for the historical museum? It seemed the only explanation of that cryptic comment. But why hadn't she just come straight out and said it?

Because if the announcement wasn't going to be made until today, not just everybody had known about the store closing—and the last thing the publisher of the *Chronicle* would do would be to take a chance of the local television station beating her newspaper to the story.

Gina closed her eyes and tried to picture the department store. It had been a while since she'd shopped there, but if her memory was accurate, the space could hardly be better suited to house a museum. Areas which had been designed for the display of merchandise would be just as good for showing off exhibits, and a soaring atrium in the center of the building brought natural but indirect light to the interior of every floor. The store was big enough to house not only every exhibit the museum currently displayed but every item currently in storage as well. The stained-glass windows from St. Francis Church would be no problem; they could have a gallery to themselves.

In addition, the building sat squarely in the middle of the downtown area—an even better location for a museum than Essie Kerrigan's house was. There was even a parking ramp right next door.

But best of all, in Gina's opinion, was the fact that nobody in their right minds would pay good money for that building. If Tyler-Royale couldn't run a profitable store in the center of downtown Lakemont, then it was dead certain nobody else could. No, Tyler-Royale couldn't sell it—but they could donate it to a good cause and save themselves a wad in taxes.

And why shouldn't that good cause be the Kerrigan County Historical Society?

The newspaper said that the CEO of Tyler-Royale had come up from Chicago to make the announcement at a press conference scheduled for ten o'clock that morning.

Since she didn't know how long Ross Clayton would be in town, Gina figured that would be her best opportunity to talk to him. All she needed, after all, was a few minutes of his time.

Not that she expected the man to make a spur-of-the-moment decision. This was hardly like making a contribution to the United Way; he couldn't donate company property without the approval of his board of directors. And even if he was in the mood to give away a building at the drop of a hat, Gina couldn't exactly take it. She didn't even want to think about the fuss it would create if she were to call a meeting of the museum's board of directors and announce that—without permission or consultation with any of them—she'd gone and acquired a new building.

But a few minutes with the CEO would be enough to set the process in motion. To give the man something to think about. And to give her a hint about whether he might act on the suggestion.

Her path toward downtown took her past Essie Kerrigan's house. Gina paused on the sidewalk in front of the museum and looked up at the three-story red brick Victorian. The building looked almost abandoned, its facade oddly blank because most of the windows had been covered from the inside to provide more room for displays.

Gina had spent the best hours of her life inside that house. As a teenager, she had visited Essie Kerrigan and listened to the old woman's tales of early life in Kerrigan County. As a college student, she'd spent weeks in the museum library doing research. As a new graduate, her first job had been as Essie's assistant—and then, eventually, her successor.

In a way, she felt like a traitor—to the house and to Essie—even to consider moving the museum away from its first and only home. The building was a part of the museum; it always had been.

But in her heart, she knew Anne Garrett had been right. She had been thinking too small. She simply hadn't wanted to let herself look too closely at the whole problem, because she had thought there was no viable alternative.

Putting a roof over the garden and the driveway would be a temporary solution for the cramped conditions, but if the plan was successful and the museum grew, in a few years they would find themselves stuck once more in exactly the same dilemma. And then they'd have nowhere to go, because the building was already landlocked, hemmed in by houses and commercial buildings.

If the museum was ever going to move, now was the time. Before they had invested hundreds of thousands of dollars in new construction. Before they tore up Essie Kerrigan's house. The house was salvageable now—a restorer would have no trouble reversing the few changes which had been made to accommodate the museum. But as soon as the work started, knocking out walls and adding a couple of wings, the house would be even more of a white elephant than the Tyler-Royale store was.

"It's all right," she whispered, as if the house were listening. "It'll be better this way. You won't be carved up after all, because a family will buy you and make you truly beautiful again."

Why the CEO had chosen to hold his press conference at the city's premiere hotel instead of in the store was beyond Gina's understanding, until she walked into the main ballroom and saw the final preparations under way. Cables and power cords snaked underfoot; lights and cameras formed a semicircle around the lectern set on a low stage at one side of the room, and people were milling everywhere. No wonder he'd wanted to keep this circus out of the store. Even though it would be closing soon, there was no sense in driving the last customers away with all the noise and confusion.

It was not exactly the place for a confidential chat, of course. But she didn't have much choice about the place or the time, so she edged into the crowd, watching intently.

Almost beside Gina, a reporter from one of the Lakemont television stations was tapping her foot as she waited for her cameraman to finish setting up. "Will you hurry up? He'll be coming in the door to the left of the podium— make sure you get that shot. And don't forget to check the microphone feed."

Gina, hoping the woman knew what she was talking about, edged toward the left side of the podium. She was standing next to the door when it opened, and she took a deep breath and stepped forward, business card in hand, to confront the man who came out onto the little stage. "Sir, I realize this is neither the time nor the place," she said, "but I'm with the Kerrigan County Historical Society, and when you have a minute I'd like to talk to you about your building. I think it would make a wonderful museum."

The man looked at her business card and shook his head. "If you mean the Tyler-Royale store, you've got the wrong man, I'm afraid."

"But you—aren't you Ross Clayton? Your picture was in the *Chronicle* this morning."

"Yes," he admitted. "But I don't exactly own the building anymore."

Gina felt her jaw go slack with shock. "You've sold it? Already?"

"In a manner of speaking."

Gina looked more closely at him and felt a trickle of apprehension run through her as she recognized him. The photo of him in this morning's paper hadn't been a particularly good one, and she only now made the connection. This was the man who'd been having lunch with Dez Kerrigan yesterday at The Maple Tree.

At that instant a tape recorder seemed to switch on inside her brain, and Gina heard in her memory what Essie had said about Dez Kerrigan.

He has no sense of history, Essie had said with a dismissive wave of her hand. *In fact, the older the building is, the better he likes knocking it down so he can replace it with some glass and steel monster.*

Dez Kerrigan was a property developer—that was what Gina should have remembered as soon as she heard his name.

A familiar and uncomfortable prickle ran up the side of her neck, and she turned her head to see exactly what she was expecting to see. Dez Kerrigan had followed Tyler-Royale's CEO onto the little stage.

"I own the building," Dez said. "Or, to be perfectly precise, what I own is the option to buy it. But I'm always ready to listen to an offer. Your place or mine?"

CHAPTER TWO

GINA couldn't believe the sheer arrogance of his question. *Your place or mine?* The very suggestion was an insult. Even if she actually *had* been staring at him yesterday at The Maple Tree—which of course she hadn't—she wouldn't have been inviting that sort of treatment. If he went around like this, propositioning every woman who happened to look in his direction...

The CEO said under his breath, "Dez, I think you're on thin ice."

Dez Kerrigan didn't seem to hear him. He glanced at his watch and then back at Gina. "I'm a little busy just now, but after the press conference we can meet at your office, or at mine. Which would you prefer?"

Gina gulped. "Office?"

"Of course." There was a speculative gleam in his eyes. "What did you think I was doing—inviting you to climb into my hot tub for a chat?" He shook his head. "Sorry, but I'd have to know you a lot better before I did that."

Gina felt as if she was scrambling across a mud puddle, trying desperately to keep her feet from sliding out from under her. She needed to do something—and fast—to get her balance back. "I, on the other hand," she said sweetly, "am quite certain that getting better acquainted wouldn't make any difference at all in how I feel about you."

His eyes, she had noticed, were not quite hazel and not quite green, but a shade that fell in between. Unless he was amused—then they looked almost like emeralds. And there was no question at the moment that he was amused.

"I suppose I should be flattered," he murmured. "Lust at first sight is a well-recognized phenomenon, of course, but—"

Even though Gina knew quite well that he was laughing at her, she still couldn't stop herself. "That is *not* what I meant. I was trying to say that I can't imagine any circumstance whatever that would get me into a hot tub with you."

"Good," Dez said crisply. "Now we both know where we stand. Do you want to talk about the building, or not?"

Gina could have hit herself in the head. How could she have gotten so distracted? "Since you've only just cut a deal to buy it, I don't see why you'd be interested in talking about selling it."

"Don't know much about the real estate market, do you? Just because there's been one deal negotiated doesn't mean there couldn't be another. Let me know if you change your mind." He stepped off to the side of the platform as Ross Clayton tapped the central microphone in the bank set up on the lectern.

Gina, fuming, headed for the exit. What was the point in sticking around? She had real work to do.

The television reporter who had been standing next to her earlier intercepted her near the door. "What was that little face-off all about?"

"Nothing at all," Gina said firmly and kept walking.

She was halfway back to the museum before she could see the faintest glimmer of humor in the whole situation. And she found herself feeling a hint of relief as well. Of course, she was still disappointed at losing the chance to acquire an ideal building, but at least she hadn't made a fool of herself by going public with her crazy plan before she'd checked it out. It would have been almighty embarrassing to have gotten the museum board excited over the possibilities and then had to go back to them and admit that her brainstorm hadn't worked.

Tyler-Royale's CEO was a pro with the press, Dez thought as he listened to the smooth voice explaining that no, the five hundred employees of the downtown store would not lose their jobs but would be absorbed into the chain's other area stores. The reporters were circling like sharks in the water, snatching bites now and then, but Ross remained perfectly calm and polite. As the questions grew more inane, Dez let his attention wander to more interesting matters.

Like the little redhead who had been lying in wait for them. Now she was something worth thinking about. First she'd turned up at The Maple Tree yesterday, having lunch with the press. He'd thought that perhaps she was a reporter too. That would account for the inspection she'd given him. She'd looked him over like a cynical searchlight—not exactly the sort of feminine once-over he was used to.

Apparently his guess had been wrong, however. *I'm with the Kerrigan County Historical Society,* she'd told Ross. And she wanted the building. *I think it would make a wonderful museum.*

Dez snorted. The trouble with the history-loving types was that they were completely impractical. The woman was totally out of touch with reality or she wouldn't have suggested anything so patently ridiculous as turning the Tyler-Royale store into a museum.

His aunt Essie would have done the same sort of thing, of course. Dez remembered visiting Essie when he was a kid, and being creeped out and fascinated all at the same time. In Essie's house, there was no telling what you might run into at the next turn. He'd found a full human skeleton in a bedroom closet once; Essie had calmly told him it was left over from the personal effects of the first doctor who'd set up practice in Kerrigan County.

And that had been well before Essie's house had formally become a museum. Though he hadn't been inside the place in at least a decade, he had no trouble imagining how much more stuff she'd collected over the years. He'd been frankly amazed, when Essie died, that they hadn't had to tear the house down in order to extricate her body from all the junk she'd collected.

At least this young woman appeared to have a little more sense than Essie had—she didn't seem to want to live in her museum. Other than that, she might as well be Essie's clone.

Apart from looks, of course. Essie had been tall and thin, seemingly all angular bone and flyaway gray hair, while this young woman was small and delicately built and rounded in all the right places. She had the big, wide-set, dark brown eyes of a street urchin—an unusual color for a redhead. Odd, how her hair had seemed sprinkled with gold under the myriad lights in the ballroom...

"Dez?" the CEO said. "I'll let you address that question."

Dez pulled himself back to the press conference, to a sea of expectant faces. What the hell was the question?

"The *Chronicle* reporter asked about your plans for the building," Ross Clayton pointed out.

I owe you one, buddy, Dez thought gratefully. At least it was an easy question—a slow pitch low and outside, easy to hit out of the park. He stepped up to the microphone. "That won't take long to explain," he said, "because I don't have any yet."

A ripple of disbelief passed over the crowd. The reporter from the newspaper waved a hand again. "You expect us to believe you bought that building without any idea what you're going to do with it?''

"I haven't bought the building," Dez pointed out. "I've bought an option to buy the building."

"What's the difference?" the reporter scoffed. "You wouldn't put out money for the fun of it. So what are you planning to do with the building?"

Another reporter, the one from the television station, waved a hand but didn't wait for a cue before she said, "Are you going to tear it down?"

"I don't know yet, Carla. I told you, I haven't made any plans at all."

"You don't know, or you just won't say?" she challenged. "Maybe the truth is you simply don't want to talk about what will happen to the building until it's too late for anyone to do anything to save it."

"Give me a break here," he said. "The announcement that the store was closing came as a surprise to me, too."

"But you leaped right in with cash in hand." It was the *Chronicle* man again.

"It wouldn't be the first time I've bought something without knowing what I'd end up doing with it."

The television reporter bored in. "Isn't it true in those cases that you've always torn the buildings down?"

"I suppose so." Dez ran over the last few years, the last dozen projects. "Yes, I think that's true. But that doesn't mean..." What had happened to the easy question, he thought irritably, the slow, low, outside pitch that should have been so simple? He felt like someone had tossed a cherry bomb at him instead. "Look, folks, I'll tell you the same thing I told the young lady from the historical society. Just because there's already been one deal doesn't mean there couldn't be another one."

"Then you'd resell the property?"

"I'd consider it. I'm a businessman—I'll consider any reasonable option that's presented to me."

"Including preserving the building?" It was the television reporter again.

"Including that." Irritation bubbled through Dez. Damn reporters; they were making it sound like he carried a sledgehammer around with him just in case he got a chance to knock something down. "As long as we're talking about preservation, though, let me give the do-gooders just one word of warning. Don't go telling me what I should do with the building unless you have the money to back up your ideas. I'm not going to take kindly to anyone nosing into my business and telling me what I should do with my property if it's *my* money you plan to spend on the project. I think that's all."

The reporters obviously realized that they'd pushed as far as was safe, and they began to trickle out of the room. A crew moved in to tear down lights and roll up cables.

In the anteroom behind the stage, Ross Clayton paused and eyed Dez with a grin. "Thanks for snatching the headlines away from the question of what's going to happen to all my employees," he said. "After the challenge you issued, that pack of wolves will be too busy ripping into you to check out anything I said."

That afternoon Gina dug out the blueprints of Essie Kerrigan's house from the attic closet where they'd been stored, and when she finished work for the day she took them home with her. Not that she was any kind of expert; expanding the museum would take not only a good architect but an engineer. Still, she might get some ideas. She might even have missed something obvious.

But when she unrolled the papers on her tiny kitchen table, she had to smother a dispirited sigh. For a little while today, it looked as if she'd found the perfect solution. It was so ideal. So sensible.

But then Dez Kerrigan had gotten in the way, and she was back at square one. Only now, as she looked at the floor plans, she was finding it difficult to focus on the possibilities. All she could see at the moment were the obstacles—the challenges which stood in the way of turning an old house into a proper museum. She had done too good a job of convincing herself that the Tyler-Royale building was the answer.

She unfolded the age-yellowed site map. Originally the house had stood alone on a full city block. Desmond Kerrigan had centered his house along one edge of his property, to leave the maximum space behind it for an elaborate garden, and he had built it facing east so it could look proudly out over the business district to the lakefront. But through the years his descendants had sold off bits and pieces of the land. The garden had been plowed up and broken into lots long ago. Later the area to each side of the house had been split off and smaller homes built there, and the street in front had been widened. The result was that the Kerrigan mansion was surrounded, hemmed in, with just a handkerchief-size lawn left in front and only a remnant of the once-grand garden behind.

It wasn't enough, Gina thought. Still, it was all they had to work with.

She weighed down the corners of the blueprints with the day's mail so she could keep looking at the drawings while she fixed herself a chicken stir-fry. Perhaps some radically new idea would leap out at her and solve the problem... For instance, what if instead of simply building over the garden, they were to excavate and add a lower level as well?

Nice idea, she concluded, but one to run past an engineer.

Would it even be possible to get heavy equipment into that small space? And how risky would it be to dig directly next to a foundation that was well over a century old?

Finally, Gina rolled up the plans and turned on the minuscule television set beside the stove. Even the news would be less depressing than her reflections at the moment.

But when the picture blinked on, the screen was filled with a shot of the Tyler-Royale store.

On the other hand, maybe it won't be less depressing.

"…and a final-close-out sale will begin next week," the female reporter—the one who had been standing next to Gina at the press conference—announced.

The anchorman shook his head sadly. "What a shame. Is there any word of what will happen to the building, Carla?"

"That question was asked at the press conference, Jason, but Mr. Kerrigan would only say that he had made no plans." She smiled coyly. "However, we did get a hint that he's negotiating a deal of some sort with the Kerrigan County Historical Society museum."

Gina's wooden spoon slipped and hot oil and vegetables surged over the edge of the pan onto her index finger. Automatically she stuck the burned tip in her mouth.

The reporter went on, "The museum's curator, Gina Haskell, was at the press conference but refused to comment—"

Gina stared unbelieving at the reporter. "I didn't refuse to comment," she protested. "I told you there was nothing going on!"

"—and when I talked to the president of the historical society just now, he would only say that it would be a crime for such a landmark building to be destroyed."

Gina put her elbows on the edge of the counter and dropped her head into her hands. They'd actually called her boss for a comment. The boss she hadn't bothered to tell about the events of the day, because her harebrained notion had come to nothing.

"Indeed it would be a crime," the anchor broke in.

The reported nodded. "However, an arrangement like that would be a first for Dez Kerrigan. He admitted today that in his entire career in property development he's never preserved a building."

"Hard to believe," the anchor said. "Keep us posted on the historical society's preservation efforts, Carla."

"*What* preservation efforts?" Gina groaned.

The phone rang. She stared at it warily, but she knew that putting off answering wasn't going to make the president of the historical society any easier to deal with. The trouble was that she didn't blame him for being furious with her. At least he hadn't told the reporter that the whole thing was news to him.

But the caller wasn't her boss. The voice on the other end of the phone was one she'd heard just once before, but she recognized it instantly. It was rich, warm—and arrogant.

"You have quite a grip on the media, don't you?" Dez accused. "Yesterday it was the newspaper, and today the TV station. What's next—rallying your troops by satellite?"

"I didn't do anything," Gina protested, but she found herself talking to a dead line.

Though she wasn't inclined to be sympathetic, she could understand why Dez Kerrigan was annoyed at being made to sound like a criminal. He'd asked for it, of course. More than ten years in the business of buying and selling property, of building and developing real estate, and he'd *never* saved a building? Still, she didn't exactly blame him for being exasperated. She was sure he had his reasons for knocking down every building that passed through his hands—inadequate though the justification might sound to ordinary people. People like her.

Being made to sound like a criminal...

Now that, she mused, might just offer some real possibilities.

It was ten in the morning, exactly twenty-four hours since their encounter in the hotel ballroom, when Gina walked into Dez Kerrigan's office.

It hadn't been easy to find him. There was no Kerrigan listed in the telephone book—not that she'd expected his home number to be published. What she had expected to find was a Kerrigan Corporation or a Kerrigan Partners or a Kerrigan-something-else. But there was nothing like that either.

Of course, she reflected, the mere fact that a man hadn't named his business after himself didn't necessarily mean the business wasn't a monument to his ego. Maybe he just liked being able to deny responsibility once in a while—and that would be harder to do with his name actually blazoned on every site he touched. Or perhaps he thought that the name had lost its impact, since it was now associated with everything from Kerrigan County itself to Kerrigan Hall over at the university, and a whole lot of stuff in between.

Eventually she located his business. He'd named it Lakemont Development, as if to say it was the only company in town that mattered. While she didn't doubt that if Dez Kerrigan had his way, his fingerprints would be all over any significant building which took place in the city, Gina thought it was hardly a less egotistical choice than naming it after himself.

Even after she'd found his business, however, she still

had a fair journey before finding Dez Kerrigan himself. Lakemont Development had offices spread all over the city, and she'd called each of them in turn, starting with the shiniest glass-and-steel tower in Lakemont and working her way down until finally a receptionist admitted, cautiously, that Mr. Kerrigan did indeed have an office in that particular building and that he was on the premises today.

Gina didn't leave her name—she just went straight over. It was only a few blocks from the museum, but she'd never noticed the building before. And no wonder it hadn't caught her eye, she thought as she approached. It looked like a converted school building—one that had been abandoned when the city's population had shifted to the suburbs. Hardly the kind of place where she'd expect to find the headquarters of somebody who played with skyscraper towers as if they were building blocks.

Inside, the building was quietly bustling. She found her way down a long corridor to Dez Kerrigan's office.

His secretary fingered Gina's business card and looked at her doubtfully. Gina wasn't surprised; the words ''historical society'' must be something of a red flag with any of Dez Kerrigan's employees.

''I don't have an appointment,'' she admitted to the secretary. ''But I imagine he's been expecting me to drop in. You may have seen on the news last night that we're negotiating a deal on the Tyler-Royale building.''

The secretary's eyes widened, but she didn't comment. She picked up the telephone, and Gina sat down in the nearest chair. She hoped she was making the point, as quietly and clearly as possible, that she wasn't going to move until she'd seen the boss.

A few minutes later the door of Dez Kerrigan's office opened. ''Well, if it isn't the media magnet in the flesh,'' he said. ''Come in.''

Gina put aside her magazine and took her time crossing the small waiting room to the inner office. He stepped back and gestured her inside with elaborate politeness.

He really was as tall as she'd thought, that day in The Maple Tree. At the press conference, she'd been too preoccupied to notice much, but now she remembered how far she'd had to look up into those odd hazel-green eyes. They didn't look like emeralds today, she noted. That was all right—she wasn't here to amuse him.

She paused just inside the door and looked around thoughtfully. "This isn't anything like I expected." The room was large—obviously it had once been a classroom—and the wall of windows and the neutral color scheme made it look larger yet. Nearly everything was various shades of gray—walls, carpet, sofa, window blinds. The desk looked like ebony. Only the art—mostly watercolors of buildings—added color. She waved a hand at a stylized drawing of a skyscraper. She recognized it—Lakemont Tower, one of the city's newest and grandest. "That's one of your projects, of course."

He nodded.

"As towers go, it's not bad. At least it has some class. But I expected you'd have your office there, with a gorgeous view over Lake Michigan."

Dez shrugged. "This office was good enough for me when I started the company, and it's still good enough. Besides, offices at the top of Lakemont Tower command a very high price. Why tie up the space myself when I can rent it out for good money?"

"Oh, yes," Gina mused. "I remember now. You told the reporters yesterday that you're the practical type."

He frowned a little. "I didn't realize you stayed around for the whole press conference."

"I didn't. But I watched the report on the late news, too.

They had more footage from the press conference then, and there you were, big as life. *'I'm a businessman,'''* she quoted. *'''I'll consider any reasonable option that's presented to me.'''*

"What about it? It's not like I'm admitting to a secret vice. Look, it's charming that you stopped by—it would have been even more charming if you'd brought a nice hazelnut coffee, but I won't hold that against you this time. However, as much as I'd like to chat, I do have things to do today."

Gina sat down on one end of the couch. "Of course you do. So I'll come to the point. I have a reasonable option for you to consider."

"*Reasonable* is a relative term. Unless you have the cash to buy me out—"

"No. I don't."

"Then please don't waste my time lecturing me about why I should preserve the Tyler-Royale building. Obviously you didn't hear the entire press conference or you'd know better than to try."

"I don't intend to do anything of the sort." She crossed her legs just so, put her elbow on the arm of the couch, propped her chin against her hand, and smiled. "I'm here this morning to give you the chance to be a hero."

Dez looked at her in disbelief. *She* was going to offer *him* a chance to be a hero? The woman had lost her mind. *If she ever had one to begin with.* "Ms. Haskell—" he began.

"Oh, call me Gina—please. I don't blame you for being upset last night," she went on with a sympathetic tone that was so palpably false that it made the air feel sticky.

"Upset?" he snorted. "I don't get upset."

"Really? Then why did you call me up and yell at me?" Dez was honestly taken aback. "I didn't yell at you."

"Oh? I suppose that's what you call calmly expressing an opinion?"

"It sure as hell is. I wasn't yelling. I admit I was annoyed at the way that pack of jackals twisted my words, especially when I thought you might have fanned the flames, but—"

She nodded. "That's what I said. You were…" It was obvious that she saw the expression on his face, for she broke off abruptly. "The news reports made you sound like King Kong, stomping around the city knocking down every building in sight. Of course you were put out by such unfair reporting."

"Lady, if I got *upset* every time a bunch of reporters took after me, I'd be living on antacids." He threw himself down on the opposite end of the couch from her. "Now what's this about you making me a hero?"

"It won't be my doing, really. I'm just here to show you the way."

She shifted around to face him, and her skirt slid up an inch, showing off a silky, slim knee. The maneuver didn't look practiced, but that only demonstrated how smooth an operator she was. "You've got about two minutes before I throw you out," Dez warned.

"Very well." With an unhurried air, she consulted her wristwatch, then settled herself more comfortably on the couch. "The media seems to have decided that you're public enemy number one. And you must admit that you've played right into their hands. Really—after all these years, and after all the projects you've been involved in, you've never yet found yourself owning a building that was worth saving?" She shook her head in apparent disbelief.

"Only this one."

She looked around the room. "And it's starting to get some age on it. Be careful, or one of these days you'll find yourself preserving a historic structure in spite of yourself."

"There's nothing historic about this building, and I'll keep it for exactly as long as it suits my purpose. Look, sweetheart, if you think I'm going to let the opinions of a few reporters keep me awake nights, you're wrong. They'll forget about saving the Tyler-Royale store just as soon as another story catches their interest. This will pass—it always does."

She kept smiling. "Sure about that, are you?"

The fact that her voice was practically dripping honey didn't lessen the threat that lay underneath the words. The antacids were starting to sound like a good idea after all.

"But why make it hard on yourself?" she went on. "You already own eight square blocks of downtown Lakemont. Or maybe it's even more than that—those were just the properties I found listed in a quick search at the county assessor's office this morning."

He had to hand it to her; she'd done her homework.

"To a tycoon, what's one block more or less?" she went on. "The media have adopted the Tyler-Royale building as their darling. If you save it, you'll be—"

"Lakemont's own superhero," he mused. "If you asked me, I'd say you've been reading too many comic books. Just for the sake of argument, exactly what kind of plan do you have in mind for saving the building? I suppose you want me to just hand it over to you?"

"Well, not to me personally, of course. But just think how marvelous you'd look if you gave it to the Kerrigan County Historical Society."

"Well, if all the goodwill in the world was resting on it, I couldn't do that. Remember? I don't own the building. I suppose I could give you the option to buy it, if I happened to be in the mood to donate something that cost me a couple of hundred thousand dollars, but what good would that do? You told me a few minutes ago you don't have any money. An option to buy is worthless if you don't have the cash to exercise it.''

''I'm sure you could help me encourage your friend the CEO to donate the building. It's not as if he wouldn't be getting anything out of the deal, after all—''

''Now you're onto something,'' Dez pointed out. ''He'd still have my two hundred grand, so he'd be happy. You'd have the building, so you'd be happy. And I'd be left holding the bag. Unfortunately for your argument, that doesn't make me look heroic. It makes me look stupid.''

''Generous,'' she corrected gently. ''Of course, you'd also be getting a nice tax deduction.''

He couldn't help but be impressed. There weren't many people who could be on the receiving end as he demolished their line of reasoning and still keep smiling like that. He wasn't sure if it was naiveté or chutzpah she was displaying, but she hadn't wilted, and that was saying something.

''And,'' she went on smoothly, ''you really shouldn't underestimate the value of improving your reputation.''

''By all means, I won't underestimate it. Doing something like that would land me on the hit list of every fundraiser and con artist in this corner of the state. You know, it would serve you right if I did hand over the option and convince Ross to sell you the building for a dollar or two. Have you actually looked at that store?''

For the first time, uncertainty flickered in her face, though she tried to mask it quickly. ''Not lately,'' she admitted.

''Well, you are in for a treat.'' He jumped up and pulled open the office door. ''Sarah, if anybody comes looking for me, just tell them that I took Ms. Haskell for a walk.''

It was only a few blocks from Dez's office to the

Tyler-Royale store, and his long legs ate up the distance. "Taking me for a *run* is more like it," Gina said, sounding breathless.

He looked disparagingly down at the strappy sandals she wore. "If you'd choose some sensible shoes, you wouldn't have so much trouble keeping up."

"And if you weren't so tall…" She stopped dead on the sidewalk in front of the main doors, looking up, and a large woman who was carrying a stack of boxes and half a dozen loaded shopping bags almost mowed her down.

Dez pulled her out of the line of traffic just in time and followed her gaze as she surveyed the front facade of the building. "What's the matter, Gina?" he hazarded. "Is it a little larger than you remembered?"

"I was just thinking it looks too busy for a store that should be closing."

Sure she was. He'd seen the way her eyes had widened as she'd taken in the sheer size of the place. But he'd play along—for a while—and let her save face.

Besides, she was right about the store being busy. People were streaming into and out of every entrance. Dez shrugged. "That happens all the time. People only realize what they have when they're told it's going to disappear. There will be a last burst of interest, and then everybody will forget about it and move on to the next store. By this time next year, if you stand on this corner and ask people what used to be here, only about half of them would even be able to tell you."

"Especially if what's here in a year is only an empty hole."

He shot a suspicious look at her, but she returned it blandly.

"Come on," Dez said. He gave the revolving door a push for her.

Just inside, a woman in a dark suit was offering samples of perfume. Gina paused and held out her wrist. Dez suspected she did it more to annoy him than because she wanted to try the scent. "The shoe department's just over there if you want to take a look," he suggested.

She sniffed delicately at the perfumed pulse point. "Oh, no. I wouldn't dream of taking up your valuable time with shoes. Or perhaps I should say I wouldn't follow your advice anyway, so I'd rather not have to listen to it."

He ushered her between the makeup counters, past fine jewelry and antique silver, to the atrium lobby. The floor was tiled in a brilliantly-colored mosaic, spirals and scallops swooping in an intricate pattern. At the center the tiny tiles formed a stylized red rose, the symbol of the department store chain. Dez led her to the heart of the rose. "Stand right here," he said.

"What's the big deal? Everybody in Lakemont has done this a million times. 'Meet me on the rose' is part of the vernacular."

"I know, I know. My mother made me report here, too. But that's not why I brought you. Look up."

For an instant he caught an odd expression in her eyes, something that looked almost like pain. What had he said to cause that reaction? Then she followed instructions, raising her eyes to the stained-glass dome seven stories above their heads.

If that didn't make her see the light, Dez thought, nothing would. He'd almost forgotten himself how immense the building was, how the rows of white-painted iron balconies seemed to go on forever, up seven floors and out for what seemed miles.

She turned back to Dez. "And the point you're trying to make is…?"

The nonchalant tone didn't fool him. "The point is that

even if you got this building for free, you couldn't handle it. You couldn't afford to keep the lights on, much less heat and cool it.''

''It's a little bigger than what we have now, of course,'' Gina conceded.

Dez stared at her for a minute, and then he started to laugh. ''Oh, that's rich! It's like saying that Lake Michigan is a little bigger than the puddle you stepped over at the curb on our way inside.''

''And it's a well-known phenomenon that when a museum expands, not only the number of visitors increases but donations do as well.''

''In your dreams.'' He extended an index finger upward and drew an imaginary circle that took in the whole building. ''Get real, Gina. Give it up. Maybe there's another building somewhere that would actually be practical.''

She shook her head. ''You don't understand, do you? Another building might be more practical, but this is the one that's captured people's hearts. This is the one that has aroused their feelings.''

Foreboding trickled through his veins.

''I'd be a fool to give up on this,'' she said, as if she savored the words.

Not as much of a fool as if you hang on to it, he wanted to say.

''It's a cause, you see—almost a crusade. It's already building momentum.'' She had the nerve to smile at him, as she added sweetly, ''And all I have to do is feed it a little.''

CHAPTER THREE

DEZ stared at her for so long that Gina thought perhaps he'd gone into a catatonic state. But even when he finally blinked and shook his head as if he was trying to clear it, he didn't say anything to her. Instead, he pulled his cell phone off his belt and without looking at it punched two keys. "Sarah, cancel my lunch meeting." He didn't wait for an answer. "Come on. Let's find a place where we can sit down and talk sense for a change."

Gina shook her head. "No, really," she said. She tried very hard not to let irony seep into her voice, and she almost succeeded. "You mustn't put yourself out for my sake. It's quite useless to try to convince me."

"It's not you I'm worried about. If you were the only one who'd be affected by this idiotic idea, I'd stand by and watch while you walked out in front of the freight train."

Well, that was brutally frank, Gina thought. "Thank you."

He frowned. "For what?"

"Confirming my suspicions that you're not nearly as unconcerned about your public image as you pretend to be."

"You think this is about my image?" He made a sound that could charitably have been called a snort. "The tearoom on the sixth floor is probably the quietest place in the building at this hour."

"And I seem to recall they have hazelnut coffee," Gina murmured.

"Hey, you can't blame me for wanting to get *something*

44

pleasant out of this. Though if you'd rather, we could stop on the fifth floor instead.''

"What's there?'' Gina asked warily.

"Hot tubs. They usually keep at least one full of water as a demonstration model.''

"On second thought, coffee sounds like a great idea.'' She paused beside the Art Deco elevator and with the tip of her index finger traced the pattern overlaid on the cool gray metal. "Elevators. Already installed. And such nice ones, too.''

"They're the originals,'' Dez countered.

"I know. They'll be like an exhibit themselves.''

"You can look at them and romanticize their history if you want, but all I see is old machinery that needs an expensive overhaul—if it isn't obsolete altogether.'' He punched at the sixth-floor button with his fist.

"They'll certainly need work if you're going to treat them that way. Surely you'll admit that they're beautiful— or isn't there a single sentimental bone in your body? Maybe I don't want you to answer that.''

"What's the big attraction of elevators, anyway?''

"We were going to have to install one. Do you have any idea how very few government grants a museum can apply for if the building isn't already completely accessible to the handicapped?''

"I can't say I've given it a lot of thought.''

"And retrofitting an elevator in an old building is extraordinarily expensive.'' That was the main reason the whole idea of building a wing onto Essie's house had come up in the first place—because there was nowhere to put a shaft. "So instead of spending the thousands of dollars we've budgeted for a new elevator, we can put that money into a fund to cover the extra utility costs.''

The elevator ran so smoothly and quietly that Gina could

hardly hear the motors. She didn't point out the fact, though; a quick glance told her that Dez already looked as if he'd like to kick something.

The beveled glass door of the tearoom rattled as he pulled it open. Though the restaurant had opened just a few minutes before, a few patrons were already there, surrounded by packages as they relaxed with drinks and pastries.

As soon as they were seated Dez leaned forward and braced his forearms on the edge of the table. "Okay," he said. "What is it that you *really* want?"

Gina raised her eyebrows at him. "Pardon me?"

"You'd be completely over your head if you got this building. You know it, and I know it. This building has close to a quarter of a million square feet of retail space. How much room do you have now? Five thousand total?"

"On the main floors, but— Wait a minute. How did you know that?"

"I make my living by judging property. Even if your head is actually as full of fluff as it seems, you can't be naive enough to think you can make that kind of jump and not fall flat on your face."

"Thanks," Gina said dryly. "It's a somewhat mixed compliment, but it's apparently the best I'm going to get."

"You're welcome. So my question is, what do you want instead? You'd have to be a fool to hold out for this building. It's not only unavailable, it's impractical. It's fifty times as big as Essie's house, give or take—you couldn't possibly use it all. Hell, with the budget you have, you probably couldn't afford to keep it all clean."

That might actually be true, Gina reflected. Not that she planned to admit it.

Her nerves hadn't completely stopped reverberating from the news that he'd paid out two hundred thousand dollars but didn't actually own a single brick. It wasn't the sheer amount of money which bothered her; the renovations on Essie's house would cost far more. But if she'd been the one spending a fifth of a million dollars, Gina thought, she'd at least have something to show for it.

Dez, on the other hand, had put out that much money with—he said—no real idea of what he'd do with his new property. It was almost as if he were using fake money from some sort of board game.

But surely even Dez Kerrigan didn't spend that kind of money lightly. Though he might not know precisely what he was going to do with the property, Gina would bet next month's rent that right now his brain was busy sorting out possibilities.

She believed him, however, when he'd said he hadn't given any thought to the building. It was nothing more than a nuisance, an obstacle that stood between him and what he really wanted—the land that lay beneath it. That was where Gina had made her original mistake—she'd failed to realize that the building wasn't the only thing for sale.

The waiter brought their coffee, Dez's hazelnut in a tall glass mug, Gina's cappuccino in a cup the size of a small mixing bowl.

She stirred her drink and said thoughtfully, "You know, it sounds to me as if you've been keeping a close eye on Essie's house."

"Why? Because I made a good guess on how big it is? No, I haven't been checking out the old home place lately. In fact, I haven't been inside it since I was about twelve."

That would have been around twenty years ago, Gina guessed. Give or take. "That was before Essie started the museum."

"No," Dez corrected, "it was before she *opened* it. She must have started collecting junk for her precious museum about the time she climbed out of her cradle. But stop trying to change the subject and let's get back to the point. This building.''

''Of course. You know, I figured when you dragged me over here that you were going to show me things like leaks in the roof and sagging walls and peeling paint.'' She eyed him over the rim of her cup. ''But you can't, can you? There's nothing wrong with it.''

''The building's in sound shape.'' He sounded as if the words had been extracted under torture.

''In fact,'' Gina mused, ''I'm betting it's so solid that it would be very difficult to tear it down. Very expensive. Very time-consuming.''

''If you're putting out a feeler to see what I'm planning to do with it, don't waste the effort. I couldn't tell you even if I wanted to, because I haven't decided. But that doesn't mean it's up for grabs. Look, Gina, we both know the building is only a diversion and you've got some other scheme in mind.''

''You may think you know—'' she began.

''So why don't you save us both some trouble and tell me what you really want? Maybe—and I'm not making any promises now, you have to understand. But maybe there's something I can do about it.''

She set her cup down very carefully, not looking at him. ''You're right about one thing. The historical museum would have trouble using all this space.''

''Good. You're starting to see reason.''

Gina went straight on. ''But there are at least a dozen small museums in Kerrigan County that are in the same sort of position we are. We don't have enough space to showcase exciting exhibits, so we have trouble drawing enough visitors even to pay the bills, much less to provide some of the extras that entice more visitors. However, if all those organizations were to throw our resources together, we could create The Museum Center.''

"A lot of museums?'' Dez's voice sounded a little hollow.

Gina nodded. "Come to one building, pay one admission charge, and visit all twelve if you like. Grandpa can wander around the historical museum and look at items from his boyhood, while Mom admires the wonderful paintings and sculptures in the art gallery, and the kids can learn about dinosaurs at the science center. All under one roof.'' She sipped her cappuccino. "I think it's perfect—and just wait till the television station hears about this one.'' She looked at him with feigned concern. "Is there something wrong with your coffee, Dez? You don't seem to be enjoying it.''

For the rest of his life, Dez thought, the mere smell of hazelnut coffee was likely to bring on one heck of a case of heartburn—because it would remind him of a petite redhead with an obsession. And not an ordinary, garden-variety obsession, either.

"You couldn't just be one of the nuts who's convinced you're really Cleopatra,'' he complained. "Oh, no—that would be much too simple. You have to be—''

Gina cleared her throat and rolled her eyes to one side. For an instant he wondered if she was about to have a seizure—how was he to predict the way her seemingly fragile mind might unravel? Then he realized that she was merely trying to direct his attention to a woman who was approaching their table.

He cast a sidelong look and had to suppress a groan. He'd called Gina a media magnet, and he'd been right—for here was that blasted television reporter who had caused all the trouble at the press conference yesterday.

Gina couldn't have planned this encounter, he reminded

himself. It hadn't been her idea to come over to the store this morning, much less to sit over coffee and negotiations in the tearoom. And there hadn't been any opportunity for her to make a phone call.

No—much as he'd like to, he couldn't blame this on her.

"Well, hello," the reporter said sweetly. "Imagine running into you two. Together."

Only Carla, he thought, could have made that one simple word sound as if she'd caught them cavorting naked in the middle of the tearoom. He half rose from his chair, making the gesture of politeness as minimal as possible. "What brings you here, Carla?"

"We're doing a series on the store, about the building's history and its architecture—that sort of thing. Do you realize that the dome is composed of over three million pieces of colored glass?"

"Thanks for counting all of them," Dez said. "It was keeping me awake nights, not knowing how many there were. If you'll excuse us, Carla—"

The reporter arched her brows. "Can I interpret that to mean you two have business to discuss? Perhaps you're talking about what's going to happen to the building?"

"Not at all," Dez said. "I'm taking a lovely lady out for coffee, that's all."

"Only coffee?" The reporter smiled. "I never thought you were so cheap, Dez. Ms. Haskell, can you give my cameraman and me some time in the next couple of days for an interview?"

Gina's gaze wandered from the reporter back to Dez. The mischief in her eyes was enough to make him wish that she really did have a Cleopatra fixation instead. Even handling an asp would be a lot less dangerous than dealing with Gina.

"I think I can fit that into my schedule," Gina murmured.

Like she wouldn't drop everything else for the opportunity.

"When would you like to arrange it?" Gina asked.

"Whenever it's convenient for you."

Dez, tired of the polite dance, growled, "Oh, why not right now?" Maybe the less time she had to prepare for an interview, the less damage she could do.

"That would be ideal," the reporter agreed. "In fact, I was going to call the museum this afternoon, so it's really been a stroke of luck to run into you. However, I wouldn't want to interfere with your...discussion."

"Oh, I think Dez is right—we're finished for the moment." Gina pushed her chair back and stood. "Thanks for the coffee, Dez. I'll see you later. Unless you'd like to come along and have the tour."

"I'd sooner have the chicken pox," he muttered.

Gina smiled brightly. "Poor dear," she said. She patted his shoulder comfortingly. "In that case, we'll just leave you here to be grumpy." She strolled away, chatting to the reporter.

Dez glumly finished his coffee and went back to his office to spend most of the afternoon shuffling paperwork. He was not going to waste time thinking about Gina Haskell, he decided. He was not going to concern himself with what she might say on camera. He was not going to contemplate how those wide, bright, pleading brown eyes would come across on television. He wasn't even going to watch the news that night.

And he certainly wasn't going to call her up to find out what had happened. He was damned if he'd give her the satisfaction.

It didn't matter, anyway. Whatever argument she might make to Carla and the television station's viewers couldn't make a fragment of difference in whatever he decided to do. No matter what sort of pressure she tried to put on him, she couldn't force him to do a single thing. He was the one who owned the building—or would own it, if he chose to. He was the one who would decide what to do with it, and he was the one who would have to come up with the money to carry out his plan. It wasn't as if he had a hand out to beg funds from the public.

But he still wished he knew what she was really up to. What was it going to take to shake loose her obsession with the Tyler-Royale building?

One thing was quite clear—she hadn't been able to conceal her shock when she'd finally realized the enormity of what she was asking for. And yet, could she really have been so shortsighted as to go after the building without having a solid plan? Without any idea whether the project she had in mind was even feasible?

You did, he reminded himself. In fact, he hadn't stopped to think at all. It had almost been a reflex action to offer to buy an option on the building, the moment he realized it was going to be for sale.

And he'd spent good money for the opportunity, too, while all Gina Haskell had invested was a little time. So if they were going to compare leaps of faith, his was certainly the longer one.

Of course, the difference was that he knew from long experience what he was doing. A square block smack in the middle of a city could always be put to good use, even if he didn't know just now exactly what that use would turn out to be. Or when it would happen. He'd taken the same leap before, and he hadn't fallen on his face yet. Someday, without a doubt, he'd seize an equally large and risky opportunity.

So perhaps Gina had simply reacted just the same way he had, and with no more planning. On the other hand, she had certainly done her homework where he was concerned. She'd known almost to the square inch how much of Lakemont he'd happened to own as of this morning. Was it reasonable to think she'd have researched him but not the building she was trying to acquire?

And yet, if she'd feigned the shock in her face just a few hours ago when she'd got her first good look at the front facade of the Tyler-Royale store and realized how enormous it really was, he'd eat the whole building. She really had been stunned for an instant—it hadn't been some sort of weird double bluff. What would have been the point, anyway?

At least, he was almost sure she hadn't been faking that reaction. The trouble was, he didn't know her well enough to take a guess as to what she really wanted.

He growled, pushed his paperwork aside, grabbed his car keys, and headed for the Kerrigan County Historical Society Museum.

He'd been truthful when he told Gina that he hadn't been inside Essie's house for the better part of two decades. But that didn't mean he hadn't driven by it on occasion. In fact, its location, just off a major street on the very edge of downtown and only a couple of blocks from his own office, made the house difficult for him to avoid.

Not that he'd tried to do that, either. He drove past it regularly, but always when he was on his way to somewhere else. Sometimes, when his mind was free, he glanced at the old house and thought about Essie and her eccentricities. Sometimes he forgot it altogether.

This time he paid much closer attention.

The front facade was shadowed, but from behind the house, the glow of sunset formed a red halo around the steep-pitched roof and the rounded cap of the tower. It was later than he'd thought. There were no lights, the doors were closed tightly, and there wasn't even a car in the driveway. The whole place was shut up tight.

That was all right, he told himself. He'd take a good look around. Tomorrow would be time enough to tackle Gina Haskell again.

He left his car under the porte cochere by the side entrance and strolled the length of the property. The back of the house was bathed in soft red light that warmed the old brick and reflected fiery red from the wavy old glass of the windowpanes. The windows looked blank and blind, but they were no longer blocked with the heavy drapes that Essie had used to protect her precious possessions; they looked instead as if they'd been boarded up from the inside.

Through the wrought-iron railing that fenced the back of the house, he surveyed the garden. There were still traces of the original, very formal arrangement, but he wasn't surprised to see that many of the plants had run wild and the flagstone paths were covered with moss. Even Essie had given up on the garden, preferring to devote her time to the interior, so it was really no wonder that the museum board hadn't been able to find the funds to keep the garden under control.

Climbing the back corner of the house and spreading over several of the blanked-out windows was a vine with glossy green leaves and stems as thick as his index finger. From the driveway he could reach a strand of it. When he pulled, a small chunk of mortar came loose with the vine's tendrils. He surveyed it thoughtfully and looked more closely at the wall.

The back door opened and Gina leaned out. "Museum hours are posted on the front porch."

He looked up from the fingernail-size chunk of mortar he was holding. "So if it's closed, why are you still here?"

"Catching up on all the work I should have been doing earlier today, when I was having coffee with you and talking to the press. Want to come in? I'll have to let you in the side door because the garden gate is rusted shut."

Dez dropped the mortar chunk into the gravel at his feet and walked back to the porte cochere.

She was waiting for him with the door held open. She'd turned on a chandelier in the entrance hall and its light added a golden sheen to her hair—but beyond the hallway he could see little more than shadows, for the only light was the red glow of the exit signs required for any place where the public gathered.

"I didn't see a car," Dez said. He pushed the door closed. The hinges creaked, but the heavy panel swung solidly into place.

"Or you wouldn't have stopped? I don't have one. I live just a few blocks away."

"You walk in this neighborhood?"

"It's no more dangerous than any other place in town. Come on back—I was just getting a soda to take up to my office."

She led the way down a short hallway. The house smelled like a museum, Dez thought. But then it always had.

Gina gave a hard push to the swinging door into the kitchen. He remembered the door from the days when he and his brother had been sent out to get themselves a snack while Essie and his parents were talking in the front parlor. Back then, the door had swung easily instead of rasping in protest as if the frame wasn't quite square.

And back then, the kitchen had been dim. Somewhere over the years the ceiling fixtures had been replaced with fluorescent ones, and now the room was bright. But the harsh bluish light didn't improve things much, Dez thought. In fact, it made the room look even dingier than he remembered—which was saying something.

Gina opened the old refrigerator and held up a can. "Would you like a Coke? There doesn't seem to be anything to go with it, though."

He took the can and popped the top. "You mean you don't still have some of those fig cookies Essie liked?"

"Sorry—I think we finally threw out the last of them. Sit down." She picked up her own can from the table which stood in the center of the room, and pulled out a chair. Curiosity sparkled in her eyes. "Was that one of the treasured memories of your childhood? Milk and cookies at Essie's?"

"Not exactly treasured, but certainly memorable." Dez took a chair across from her. "I'll never forget those rock-hard fig cookies—it took a full glass of milk to soak up each one. Is her cookie jar still around somewhere?"

"If you mean the chubby little blue-glazed pot, yes. It's upstairs, on display."

"A cookie jar?" He didn't try to keep the incredulity out of his voice. "Why? Because it was Essie's?"

"Not exactly. It wasn't really intended to be a cookie jar, you know—it's a prize piece of pottery fired in the first kiln built in Kerrigan County."

"Figures," Dez said. "No wonder the cookies dried out."

"Well, that wasn't entirely the fault of the jar, because the cookies had a head start before they ever got that far. Essie bought them in bulk at the day-old bakery store since they cost less there."

"She bought cheap, already-stale cookies, but she stored them in an old pot she probably paid a fortune for."

"She didn't, actually. But even if she had, it would have been worth it. As far as we can figure out, it's the only piece of that potter's work which has survived."

Dez shook his head. "Essie hadn't changed much, obviously."

"We all have soft spots, things that are particularly precious to us."

He wasn't going to get a better opening, Dez thought. "And this museum is one of yours."

She didn't bother to answer, just raised her soda can in a sort of half salute.

He leaned an elbow on the table. "I can already see why you want to move the museum out of the house, of course."

Gina raised an eyebrow. "Oh, really? Why?"

He pointed at the ceiling, where a crack ran diagonally across the room. "Things like that. This house must be settling every which way."

"On the contrary. That crack has been there as long as I remember. It's part of the character of the house. Practically an old friend."

"How long is it since you made its acquaintance?"

"Ten or twelve years." She sounded almost wary.

She must have been barely in her teens, he thought. "How did you get to know Essie well enough to be invited into her kitchen?"

"She was still teaching history when I was in middle school."

It wasn't exactly an answer to the question, he noted. But it seemed to Dez that she'd said all she intended to. "And the creaky swinging door? I suppose you're going to say it's always been like that, too."

"Well, it might not have been creaky in your time," she

pointed out. "Though for all I know, the hinges are sprung because you used to work up an appetite for Essie's fig cookies by using it as a climbing gym."

"How did you know— Essie must have told you."

"As a matter of fact, she didn't. If she had realized you were using the door as a playground ride, she'd have put a stop to it. I said it because it just seemed to be the sort of thing you'd do."

"Because it's destructive, I suppose you mean."

"You said that—I didn't. But if your hand fits in that particular cookie jar—"

"Then I have to claim it? So if the house is in such great shape, why are you anxious to move?"

"Oh, I'm sure you don't need me to explain that."

"That's true enough. I can think of at least sixteen reasons, ranging from the fact that you have no place to put a parking lot for guests to the fact that the lack of air circulation in here can't be good for your priceless collections. I just wondered which of the sixteen was most important to you."

"Be careful," Gina murmured. "You're only encouraging me to want the Tyler-Royale building more and more."

"That building is a ridiculous stretch for you and we both know it. What about St. Francis Church?"

"Meaning what?" She sounded even more wary. "I've already been offered the windows, but I don't have room for them. Unless I get the Tyler-Royale building—"

He cut her off almost mid-word. "You could use the church for your museum. There's already a nice big parking lot and an elevator. You can even leave the windows right where they are."

She looked thoughtful.

Now we're getting somewhere. He pressed the advantage.

"Get real about the Tyler-Royale building, and let's start talking about St. Francis Church instead."

"I should have known you owned that, too. Funny—it didn't show up on the list this morning."

He wasn't about to admit why she hadn't found a record of the sale. "Good. Now that you see the sense in using that building instead—"

"Whoa. I didn't say anything of the sort. I was just wondering why you weren't planning to bulldoze the stained-glass windows along with the rest of the building." She tapped her forehead lightly with the back of her hand. "Oh, that was dumb. Obviously saving them wasn't your idea. What happened? An activist group in the parish insisted, as a condition of the sale?"

He ignored her. "You could kill two birds with one stone. Have your new museum building *and* the windows, without even the cost of moving them."

She shook her head. "I've been all through the church, when I was appraising the windows. It isn't enough bigger than what we have now to be worth the effort of moving everything we own."

Was the woman nuts? Or hadn't he made himself clear? "I'm willing to give it to you, Gina, if you'll just let go of the crazy notion that you can manage to end up with the Tyler-Royale building."

"I know you're offering to give it to me," she murmured. "That's what makes the whole thing so interesting, you see. St. Francis as an opening offer, free and clear. I wonder how much more you'll be willing to give me before it's over."

And she smiled at him.

CHAPTER FOUR

GINA let the silence draw out for a few seconds as she sipped her Coke. She could almost see the calculations going on inside Dez's head. "I really must get back to work now," she murmured. "But feel free to look around. My office is right at the top of the attic stairs. Just let me know when you're finished, and I'll come down and lock up."

He didn't answer. He moved suddenly, and she thought for an instant that he was going to reach out a hand to stop her, but he seemed to think better of it.

Gina climbed the open staircase from the main floor, turning on the lights as she went. Normally she didn't bother, because she knew every inch of the house so well she could walk through it blindfolded. But if Dez took her up on the invitation to look around, he might not even know where to look for the light switches. Since the house had been built well before electricity was common in Lakemont, some of the wiring had ended up in pretty odd locations.

Essie had run the museum from a desk in her bedroom, but now that room, too, was open to the public. Gina had done her best to reproduce an old-time photo studio there, choosing from a stash of items that Essie had bought at auction years ago, after a longtime business had closed downtown. But though the room was the largest on that floor, the artifacts were cramped and the setting not quite convincing. And some of the best items were still in crates in the basement, because they were too large to fit into the display.

"If we just had more room," she muttered as she passed the door and went on up the narrow, winding stairway which led to the attic. Space there was less precious, so she could spread out her work without feeling as if she was stealing exhibit possibilities from the museum. And having an office right at the top of the house had an extra advantage—not as many people were willing to climb all the way up to talk to her.

Her office was, as she'd told Dez, literally at the top of the attic stairs, where the peak of the roof was highest. She'd never gotten around to building walls or even ordering an office cubicle; she'd simply pushed trunks and boxes aside to leave enough room for a desk and a folding table. The lamp on her desk cast a pool of light to work by and threw mysterious shadows across the rest of the room, turning a dress form into a misshapen monster, gleaming dully off a tarnished silver candelabra, and reflecting from the age-darkened mirror of the old coatrack which stood at the end of her desk. The only thing she'd managed to do to mark her territory was to put out her favorite coffee cup and hang her college diploma on one of the coatrack's hooks.

She set down her soda can and buried herself once more in trying to plan a budget—not an easy task since she had no real idea of where the museum would be located at this time next year. She had almost forgotten Dez when she heard the narrow stairs creak under his weight and saw his head appear just above the railing in front of her desk.

He stopped a few steps down from the top so his face was level with hers as she sat at her desk, and looked around at the attic miscellany. "Now I see why you want more space."

Gina didn't look up from the budget figures she was crunching. "Congratulations. You win first prize for perception. However, if you think this is bad, you should see the basement.''

''You store stuff in the basement?''

''It's a little musty, but it's perfectly dry. Any better ideas? Say, for instance, the storage rooms on the lower level of—''

''Don't say it.'' He came up the last few steps and around the railing. ''If everything Essie owned is so precious to the museum—''

Gina pulled the calculator over and began adding up a row of figures. ''Did I say that?''

''Then what about the house itself? She tried to save everything else—but what's going to happen to the house when you move out?''

''It will be preserved.''

''I see. That's the reason you want the Tyler-Royale building—because this whole house will fit inside the atrium, right on top of the rose, and leave room to spare.''

He was exaggerating, of course, and Gina refused to rise to the bait. ''No, I'm not planning to move it. It will be a home again.''

''For whom? You?''

She looked up at that. ''Me? What would I do with the place?''·

Dez shrugged. ''It seemed logical. You appear to be one of the few people who wouldn't be put off by the neighborhood.''

''I'm not trying to move the museum just so I can personally get my hands on this house. It's a great house—but I don't have time to do all the work it needs.''

''At least you're admitting it needs work.'' He leaned a hip against the stair railing. It creaked ominously and he moved, without apparent haste, to prop himself against the coatrack instead.

Was he joking? "Of course it needs work. The kitchen's fine as a staff room for now, but no serious cook could put up with it for long. Essie was different—she was used to it."

He looked at her curiously. "You're talking about remodeling."

"I'd say stripping a room to the walls and starting over is more than simple remodeling, but you can call it whatever you want."

"So you're a serious cook."

"I could be," Gina admitted cautiously, "if I had time and energy. But if you mean, have I designed my dream kitchen to fit into that space, no. The house is much too large for one person—even with all her possessions, Essie rattled around in it."

"So who's going to live here, if it isn't you?"

Was there more than casual interest in his voice? "How should I know? Some family will buy it and fix it up, I suppose."

Dez shook his head. "Considering the rest of the houses around here, it's far more likely to end up cut into makeshift apartments. Or else it'll be a burned-out hulk."

Gina shook her head. "If you're trying to convince me that it's my civic duty to stay right here and anchor the neighborhood because that's what Essie wanted—"

"I wondered if you'd admit that."

Gina didn't pause. "I'm not admitting anything. How could you possibly know what Essie intended? You never came around to see her."

"Did you hang around here enough to meet all her visitors?"

As a matter of fact, yes. "Surely if you'd been visiting on a regular basis, you would know how much I was hanging around,'' she said sweetly. ''Besides, you told me you hadn't been inside the house in twenty years.''

''Oh. I forgot I said that.''

''Perhaps you should take notes. At any rate, before you start telling me what Essie would have wanted, I suggest you think twice.''

''You, on the other hand, know all about what Essie wanted. And what she didn't want.''

It wasn't a question, and his tone was both silky and insinuating.

Gina said warily, ''I'm the one who was here. You weren't.''

He sat down on the corner of the desk. ''It's an interesting question, you know. What exactly you found so absorbing about an old woman and all her collections.''

As if I'm going to explain it to you. ''If you're suggesting that I cozied up with Essie for what I could get out of her—''

''My goodness, we're touchy.''

Yes, Gina thought. *We are.*

''Though from all appearances, if that's what you were doing, you weren't very successful.'' His gaze flicked around the office space, at the worn top of the old wooden desk, at the filing cabinet with the dented drawer front. ''I can't imagine the museum pays you very well. Perhaps that explains why you want a different building.''

''As an excuse to raise funds so I can skim a little off the top? The way your mind works is quite interesting.''

''But I'm not the one who mentioned stealing.'' His voice was like satin.

Gina's hand clenched on her pencil, and she forced her muscles to relax. *Time to change the subject.* ''As far as the house is concerned, Essie was a realist.''

''Up to a point, I'm sure she was. But that doesn't mean

she'd be pleased at seeing it turned into a boardinghouse or a bordello. But frankly I can't see much other future for it—anyone who has the money it would take isn't going to invest in a house in this neighborhood. They'd never be able to resell it.''

"Why would they want to? And for your information, at least three times a week museum guests comment about how beautiful the house is and how much they'd like to own it.''

"And they probably think they mean it, too,'' Dez agreed. "Right up to the point where you would actually offer to sell it to them. Then they'd turn just as green as you did this morning when you realized what a big chunk of real estate the Tyler-Royale building represents, and how far above your head you were reaching.''

"I did not turn green. In any case, if you're so worried about what happens to Essie's house, there's an easy solution.'' Gina pushed the calculator aside. "Buy it yourself.''

"This house? Me? Why would I want it?''

"A better question is, why wouldn't you?'' she murmured, and picked up her pencil again.

"My dear girl, if you're going to start in on me about why I should honor the Kerrigan heritage by maintaining the family estate, as if it were some stately home listed on the National Register...''

"Of course not. That would be silly.''

"Good. At least you haven't gone quite over the brink and started worshiping anything that's mildly old, regardless of actual value.''

"I don't mean that it would be silly to value the family heritage,'' she mused. "Expecting you to appreciate and honor it, on the other hand—*that's* what would be silly. I just meant that buying the house must make perfect sense from your point of view." She looked straight at him. "Why not snap it up? You seem to want to own everything else."

Dusk had settled around the museum by the time Gina locked the side door behind Dez. She turned off the lights in the entrance hall, but she didn't go back up to her office. Instead, she stood at the bottom of the long stairway, one hand caressing the satin-smooth walnut railing where it curved into the newel post, thinking.

Was Dez right? Had she been absurdly optimistic about what would happen to Essie's house if the museum moved out of it?

Or was she simply being foolish now even to give it a thought?

"Your responsibility is to the museum," she reminded herself. "It's not to Essie anymore."

For many years the two things—Essie and her museum—had been inseparable. But now, with Essie gone...what if the choice which produced the best outcome for the museum was no longer what Essie would have wished?

"Then you have to do what's right for the museum," Gina told herself firmly. "That's your job."

But though that was without question true, it didn't feel comfortable. The very idea of going against what Essie would have wanted, what Essie would have thought, sent flutters of misgiving down every nerve. After everything Essie had done for her, Gina felt as if she was turning her back on her mentor. No, worse than that. It felt as if she were sticking out her tongue and blowing a raspberry.

Just as the kids in middle school had done on occasion— but only when Essie couldn't see them.

Old Maid Essie, the kids had called her—behind her

back, of course. They had thought her stern and humorless, and in her classroom, there was no modern nonsense about how the best way for thirteen-year-olds to learn about the Pilgrims was to dress up in black suits and hop from one desk to another, pretending that one was the *Mayflower* and the other Plymouth Rock. Essie Kerrigan taught history— and grumble though her students might about her methods, they learned it.

Gina had heard the stories and the warnings before she'd ever entered Essie Kerrigan's classroom, and so from the very first day she'd kept her head down and tried not to draw attention to herself. Without much success—though exactly why Miss Kerrigan had first taken an interest in her, Gina had never known. She certainly hadn't invited curiosity in the classroom.

And now she was repaying Essie's interest and Essie's confidence in her by destroying the old woman's house. Or at least that was the way Dez Kerrigan had tried to make it sound.

As if he cared what happened to Essie's house. The question would probably never have occurred to him if she'd accepted his offer of St. Francis Church as a substitute. But as soon as she had turned that down, he'd immediately shifted tactics—trying, with an armload of guilt, to con her into staying exactly where she was.

Down deep, Gina knew, his real intention hadn't changed at all. She wondered just how far he'd go in his attempt to get her distracted from the Tyler-Royale building.

Well, one thing was sure—when it came to destruction, Dez Kerrigan knew what he was talking about. It would take a miracle to save the Tyler-Royale building.

That must be why he hadn't even asked about her interview this afternoon—because he had already made up his mind.

She wondered exactly what he'd decided to do with the land, and how long it would take him to start moving.

Dez had absolutely no intention of watching the late news. No matter what Gina had said to Carla and the camera crew that afternoon, it couldn't make any difference to him. His time would be much better spent in reviewing the preliminary reports that he'd brought home with him, and then doing some serious thinking. Maybe even sketching out a design or two to pass along to the architects, just to give them some direction.

At any rate, whatever Gina Haskell did, it wasn't his problem. He'd handed her the best option anywhere around when he'd offered her St. Francis Church. If she didn't have the good sense to grab it, that wasn't his problem.

Though as a matter of fact it *was* his problem, he admitted, because now he had to decide what to do with the darned thing.

On the other hand, perhaps it would be smart to at least see what she was up to…

He put down his sketch pad and reached for the remote control. The instant he turned on the television, Gina's face—all earnestness and wide brown eyes—filled the screen.

The cameraman must have been mesmerized, Dez thought, judging by the way he'd focused in tight on her eyes and cut the reporter out of the picture entirely. Dez didn't blame him. Those eyes were big enough and deep enough to drown a man's common sense.

And he didn't have to look far for an example. Half a dozen times today he'd found himself wishing she'd chosen the hot tub instead of the tearoom this morning—and not just because they'd have escaped Carla, either.

He needed his head examined, that was all there was to it.

"Of course," Gina was saying soberly, "I think it would make a wonderful museum. But perhaps I'm prejudiced, since that's my job. At any rate, it's not up to me to make the choice. The building belongs to Dez Kerrigan, and he'll be the one who decides what happens to it."

Dez's jaw dropped. She was actually admitting—in public, on television—that he was the one in charge and she had nothing to say about it?

"But I'm sure everyone in Lakemont has an opinion about it, just as I do," she went on. "And I hope they'll all let Mr. Kerrigan know how they feel."

I should have known she wouldn't let me off the hook that easily.

"Now that's a thought," Carla said. "Perhaps we should find out what the man on the street thinks."

The tape cut away to show Carla outside the main entrance of Tyler-Royale, stopping every passerby to ask what he or she thought should be done with the building.

Turn it into a hotel, one said. Make it a flea market, said another.

Dez rolled his eyes.

"A jail," one woman said triumphantly. "Just think how many prisoners it would hold!"

Carla conceded that was indeed true. Dez had to give her credit for keeping a straight face as she turned back to the camera. "Tomorrow we'll delve further into the history of the building," she said. "And we'll take a closeup look at the ornamentation which covers it, and find out from Gina Haskell what all that decoration means, and why it's there."

The camera focused once more on Gina as she pointed up at the roofline of the building. Then the lens followed her gesture upward, zooming in on a face molded into a medallion which looked out over the city from a perch along the very top edge of the terra-cotta frieze.

What a waste of money, putting it way up where nobody can even see it without binoculars.

It was too bad, Dez thought, that the damn medallion hadn't chosen that instant to let go of the perch where it had been glued for a hundred years. Not that he *really* wanted to see Gina Haskell squashed on the sidewalk, but the crash would certainly have made the point that no matter how many grand ideas were floating around, sooner or later somebody would have to be practical.

A jail. He snorted and went back to his sketch pad.

Of all the aspects of her job, the one Gina liked least was the social obligation that came with being not only the director of the museum but its entire public relations department and the head fund-raiser. Essie had never quite understood her hesitation—but then Essie had been strong-arming her friends into donating money and volunteering time. Gina was still, for the most part, approaching strangers.

A *lot* of strangers, she realized when she got out of the cab in front of Anne Garrett's Tudor house on Sunday evening. The street was choked with cars even though there was a temporary valet stand set up at the curb, and there was a steady stream of party-goers on the sidewalk.

She paid the driver and joined the parade of guests, trying not to think about how much she hated cocktail parties and how useless they all seemed to be. An entire evening of mumbled names and inane remarks that no one ever listened to anyway, even if the noise level wasn't such to prevent easy comprehension… But at least she could exchange business cards, and then when the museum board decided which direction to move, she could call all these people and remind them of where they'd met.

But Anne Garrett's party was different, and not only because the surroundings were grander than Gina had encountered before. She was barely inside the front door, still admiring the linen-fold paneling and the coffered ceiling of the entrance hall as she waited her turn to go into the big room beyond, when a man standing in the far corner of the hallway almost pushed aside his companion and came over to her.

Gina saw the look on his face and braced herself. "Hello, Mr. Conklin."

Jim Conklin didn't bother with the niceties. "What in hell do you think you're doing these days?" he demanded. "Cavorting all over television and making deals right and left without even asking a by-your-leave… The board hired you to be director of the museum, not dictator-in-chief."

Dictator-in-chief. That was cute, Gina admitted. Unfortunately, Jim Conklin hadn't meant it as a joke.

"Have you even talked to the president?" he growled.

"Not yet," Gina admitted. "I've been trying to reach him. However, I'll be happy to give you and all the other members of the board a full report at next week's meeting."

He snorted. "After you've got everything lined up the way you want it, I suppose."

No—because if I waited that long, it would be well into the next century. She started to say that she would have already called a special meeting if there had been anything to report, but Jim Conklin didn't give her a chance.

"Well, if you expect the board to rubber-stamp your decisions this time," he went on irritably, "think again. I always did say we made a mistake, giving you the job just because Essie wanted you to have it. You're too much like her—thinking the museum's your own pet project. Swapping buildings right and left..."

Over his shoulder, Gina caught a glimpse of a tall blond woman who seemed to be craning her neck in Gina's direction. Not that Jim Conklin wasn't giving everyone within twenty feet plenty of reason to stare—but this woman looked vaguely familiar. From some other cocktail party, probably, Gina told herself. After a while, she'd found, all the parties—and all the people—tended to run together until it was difficult to remember who she had met and when.

"Will you pay attention when I'm talking to you?" Jim Conklin snapped.

Gina had had enough. "When you're *talking,* yes," she said softly. "So if you'd like to stop by my office in the next few days so we can discuss this rationally instead of shouting about it—"

"I'm a working man. I can't take time off to run over to the museum because you want to chitchat. I've already spent precious time arranging for an expert to come to the board meeting next week to talk about our ideas for expansion, and then I find out on the nightly news that you've set aside the whole idea of building new wings in favor of adopting the biggest white elephant Kerrigan County's ever seen."

A voice behind Gina said lazily, "I think I'd consider that a vote against moving the museum."

She wheeled around, and Dez reached for her hand and closed her fingers around the stem of a champagne flute. "You look as if you could use this, my dear."

Gina fleetingly thought about *using* it to rinse his hair, but he'd already looked on past her to Jim Conklin. "You'll excuse us, sir, I'm sure. Gina and I have so many things to settle."

She could have braced her feet and resisted the gentle tug on her arm, but what was the point? At least—judging from previous experience—Dez wasn't likely to air their quarrel for the world to listen in on, which made a nice change from Jim Conklin.

Dez moved slowly through the crowd. When they were halfway across the big living room, a man stepped out into Dez's path, a wide grin on his face. "As long as you're soliciting opinions on your building, Kerrigan, I think you should make it an amusement park. Gut the inside and put up roller coasters. It's a natural—you'd never have to shut down because of weather." He laughed merrily and without waiting for an answer he moved out of the way.

Oh, dear, Gina thought. What was it Dez had said? *Gina and I have so many things to settle...* She had a feeling she wasn't going to like this at all.

She tried to dawdle, but Dez seemed able to find a path where Gina would have sworn there wasn't one. A tap on the shoulder, a word, and the way parted before them. Before she knew it, they had bypassed the portable bar set up at the far end of the living room and he'd led her out into a solarium beyond.

"Just how far are you planning to take me?" she asked finally. "Because if we're going much further, perhaps I should stop at home and pack a bag."

Dez stopped beside a metal cart full of blooming orchids and swung her around to face him. "Oh, what you're wearing will be good enough." His gaze traveled down to her toes, and then back up. "I see your taste in shoes hasn't improved. And obviously I was wrong about one of my guesses."

"Only one? I'd counted a dozen miscalculations at least."

"My speculation about how much the museum pays you

must have been way off—if your salary lets you dress like that.''

If he thought she was going to explain to him how she managed life on a museum director's salary, he was dead wrong. She ran a hand over the shoulder of her cream-colored dress. "Thank you." She kept her voice as sweet as she could. "And yes, you're right—it is a designer label. Quite unique, in fact." *Especially after I brought it home from the thrift shop and altered it to fit me.*

"I gather that was one of your board members," Dez said. "There appears to be some dissension in the ranks."

Gina sipped her champagne. "Isn't there always? No group of people always agrees, and when you're dealing with a governing body where every individual thinks he's the boss... Well, you must have found that out from dealing with your own board of directors.''

"I don't have one. There really is only one boss in my business.''

"No wonder you can toss around money like confetti," Gina muttered.

"At least it's my money. You, on the other hand, toss around cheap ideas and really gum up the works. *I hope they'll all let Mr. Kerrigan know how they feel,*" he mimicked. "Congratulations. They listened."

"You mean the guy who proposed the amusement park?''

"That is the least of the schemes. It has also been suggested that I turn it into a grain elevator—"

"It's not close enough to the docks to be practical," Gina murmured, and then thought better of it when she saw his expression. "Sorry."

Dez plowed on. "—Or a car dealership, an artists' colony, a skateboard ramp, or a factory to grow hydroponic tomatoes. My favorite was the idea of making it into a zoo—but only if I can personally, and very slowly, feed you to the lions. Everywhere I've gone for the last two days, someone has another zany idea of what I should do with my building.''

"I sort of like the artists' colony," Gina offered. "Nice big studios with lots of natural light. Of course, most artists don't have much money."

"The only thing no one has mentioned, in fact, is a museum. Does that give you a clue how the thinking is running?''

"Well," she said reasonably, "if this has become Lakemont's newest party game, then the kookier the ideas, the better people like them. And since turning it into a museum actually makes sense, of course that's the last thing anyone would suggest to you."

He growled. "Then I come here tonight and find out that you're not even serious.''

Gina frowned. "How did you reach that conclusion?"

"Because you and your board member were talking about building wings onto Essie's house. Wings! Not only is that just about the worst idea I've ever heard, but—"

"If you're worried about the house, Dez, I've already told you how you can protect it."

"Buy it? No, thanks. Besides, it doesn't sound like your board of directors would be willing to sell."

"Don't judge them all by Jim Conklin. Some of the others are less excited than he is by the idea of putting on an addition or two."

"Sounds like at least some of them have their heads on straight."

"Well, it *would* be a shame to build a cube sided in white vinyl on the front lawn and cover up the tower."

Dez looked at her with narrowed eyes, and Gina thought perhaps she'd gone just a bit too far. He must realize she wouldn't do anything to Essie's house that would actually destroy it.

"Building onto that house would be a damn-fool thing to do." His voice was flat.

Gina shrugged. "Then offer me some options. And don't start with St. Francis Church this time."

Through the door and down the two steps into the solarium came the tall blonde who had been eyeing Gina in the front hall. "I'm so sorry to interrupt," she said, sounding anything but apologetic. "But I simply had to be certain. It really is you, isn't it, Gina?"

Gina had learned the hard way, long ago, not to bluff about remembering someone. There were too many trip wires, too many pitfalls. "I'm afraid I don't recall you."

"Oh, you wouldn't, I'm sure." The blonde approached and held out a hand. "Jennifer Carleton—we were in school together. We must have been about thirteen. I've changed a bit since then, no doubt."

Gina remembered the woman, though she wouldn't have said they were in school *together*. She would have called it being in school *at the same time*—because she couldn't think of a single class or activity or even conversation that she and Jennifer Carleton had ever shared. "That's been a long time ago."

Jennifer smiled. Her teeth were very white and very straight, and for just an instant they looked as if the edges had been filed sharp. "Yes, and you had such a lot on your mind at the time... You haven't changed much at all, I must say. It was your dress that first caught my eye tonight, you know. It's just—exactly—like one I used to wear."

"What a coincidence." Gina kept both her gaze and her voice level.

"Isn't it, though? I'm quite unhappy with the designer. He assured me it was one of a kind. I wonder what ever happened to mine... Oh, I remember now. I donated it to the Salvation Army thrift store. Dez, when you're free..." *When you've cut yourself loose from this nuisance,* her tone said.

"Oh, don't let me keep you waiting," Gina said gently. "Dez was so anxious to get me to himself that I haven't even had a chance to say hello to my hostess yet." With her head high, she crossed the solarium.

Gina climbed the steps, watching from the corner of her eye as Jennifer laid a hand on Dez's arm. "I need to talk to you about the plans for the Carousel Ball," Jennifer said in an intimate undertone. "One of the committee members thought it would be fun to hold the dance in the Tyler-Royale atrium this year. But she didn't feel she knew you well enough to ask, so I was delegated to do the dirty work." She laughed merrily.

Public dance hall. There's another possibility for you, Dez.

It was the first time in her life that Gina had looked out across a cocktail party crowd with a feeling of relief and then plunged into the noise with actual enthusiasm. She'd just have to keep an eye out to make sure she didn't run headlong into either Jim Conklin or Jennifer Carleton again. Once in an evening was enough.

It was bound to happen sometime, Gina told herself philosophically. *If you're going to buy clothes at thrift shops and wear them to events like this...* The only wonder, she supposed, was that it hadn't happened before. Unless, of course, the previous owners of her other clothes had simply been less certain, or more tactful, than Jennifer Carleton was.

Anne Garrett was nowhere in sight, so Gina swapped her champagne flute for a fresh one and started to circulate through the crowd.

She was so busy watching out for Jim Conklin and Jennifer Carleton that she was almost face-to-face with Tyler-Royale's CEO before she spotted him. In fact, she bumped his elbow while she was reaching for a tidbit from the sumptuous array on the table. "Sorry," she said automatically. "I've never seen an ice carving that shape before. And it's practical, too—carving a shell and using it as a bowl to hold the shrimp." Then she looked up. "Mr. Clayton—you're still in town?"

That was pretty stupid, she told herself. *Obviously he's not in Tokyo.*

He smiled. "And I'll be here for quite a while yet, I'm afraid. There's a mountain of paperwork that goes along with closing a store. It's one of the reasons we hate to close one."

"I can imagine."

"And the presence of senior management helps to reassure our employees that we really do mean to take care of them, not toss them out in the cold. I'm glad to run into you again, though. I need to thank you."

"For what?" Gina said uncertainly.

"For the sudden rush of customers we've experienced. In the last few days foot traffic has increased by thirty percent, and a good two-thirds of our visitors say they want the store preserved just like the lady from the museum was talking about on television."

Gina frowned. "So does that mean you've decided to keep it open?"

"Oh, no." His voice was dry. "I said foot traffic was up, not sales. It's been very interesting, however. Everyone has a suggestion about what should happen to the building. All the sales associates have started collecting them, and whenever I hear a particularly good one, I call Dez and leave it on his voice mail."

"He isn't answering his phone anymore?"

"He stopped sometime yesterday, though I can only speculate as to why. So I don't know yet how he reacted to the idea of turning it into the world's biggest recycling center."

Anne Garrett reached between them for a tiny sandwich. "Hi, Ross—thanks for sending over your ice sculptor. I hope you're not laying him off when the store closes, but if you are, I want his phone number. Gina—I'm glad you came, because we need to talk." She shook her head in what looked like amazement. "You know, I never dreamed you'd be so good at taking advice."

Gina asked warily, "Is that a problem?"

Dez reached over Gina's shoulder and speared a shrimp with a plastic skewer. "Good at taking advice? *Gina?* Now this I have to hear."

CHAPTER FIVE

GINA tried to catch Anne's eye to telegraph a message. *Whatever's going on, this isn't the time to discuss it.* But Anne wasn't looking at her. She was smiling up at Dez.

"I hear," Anne said calmly, "that you're thinking of building a ski slope inside the Tyler-Royale building. Climate controlled, year-round..."

Dez assumed the air of a wounded puppy. "If you want me to go away, Anne, all you have to do is ask. You don't have to kick me when I'm down."

"Oh, it's good for you to get a slug in the ego every now and then," Anne said.

Gina wanted to nod agreement, but she figured it would be a lot wiser to remain invisible.

"So what advice have you been handing out?" Dez wondered.

"Not to mind other people's business," Anne said sweetly.

"And you think Gina listened too well? That's a laugh. But I can take a hint."

"That's the first evidence I've seen of it," Anne muttered.

Dez piled up a plateful of snacks. "I think I'll go see if I can find that board member again. Conklin? Is that what you said his name was, Gina?"

Gina didn't much care who he went looking for, as long as he went. In any case, she thought, he was probably only trying to get a rise out of her by making her think he was going to compare notes with Jim Conklin. The moment he was out of earshot, she turned to Anne. "What are you talking about? What's the problem?"

"I wouldn't exactly call it a problem. I just thought I should tell you that the advice you apparently acted on didn't happen to be the same advice I was giving."

Gina was still puzzled. "You said I should be sure to read the newspaper. I just put two and two together."

"And you got sixteen. I said you should think bigger, but it never occurred to me that you might take on Goliath."

"But the Tyler-Royale story was right there on the front page—"

Anne nodded. "Yes, it was. You couldn't miss it. But I never dreamed you'd think that was what I was talking about."

Gina's ears were buzzing as if her brain had somehow gone out of tune. Anne *hadn't* been tipping her off about the department store? *Hadn't* been suggesting that she go after it?

"Apparently you didn't get past the front page that day," Anne went on.

Gina's throat was dry. "I flipped through the whole paper. But I thought it was so obvious that you were hinting about the store closing, but you couldn't tell me because it might ruin your exclusive. So—if that's not what you meant—what *were* you talking about?"

"There was a column on the editorial page about the museum. I enjoyed my tour so much that I wrote a piece about Kerrigan County's hidden treasure chest, suggesting that everybody in town should make a visit."

"I never saw it." *I was so caught up in thinking about Tyler-Royale...* "Visits have been up a bit, but I just assumed that was because of the controversy."

"No doubt it is," Anne admitted. "My story was just a

pleasant little rambling about how much fun our visit had been. And the headline could certainly have been better. If it had actually named the museum, it would have been more likely to catch your eye. But editorial page headlines are one of the things I don't have much control over.''

"Even if you wrote the story?" Gina hardly heard her own words; she was still too stunned by the news.

"Even then. Of course, if I'd realized when I wrote it that you were going to be starting a fund-raising drive, I would have done it a little differently, but since the column was already set up before our lunch date, it was too late to change anything.''

Gina was hardly listening. "But if you weren't suggesting I go after the Tyler-Royale building…"

"No, I'm afraid even I wasn't thinking on quite such a scale. That one was entirely your idea, Gina.''

"What a colossal blunder." Gina's voice was little more than a whisper; she suddenly was having incredible trouble drawing a full breath. How could she have been such an idiot?

"Or else it's sheer genius," Anne mused. "I'll be as interested as everybody else in town to see which it turns out to be. In the meantime, if you're to have any chance at all, you really need to start asking for money while people are in the mood to give. The first few pledges and volunteer workers will be easy to find, but you aren't going to get much further without an organized effort. How about lunch sometime next week to get things rolling?''

"I don't think so," Gina managed. "If I ask for money to turn that building into a museum, and then I don't get the building—"

Anne shook her head. "No, no. You're sounding pessimistic, and that's no way to accomplish anything. We'll raise funds for museum expansion, with no promises of exactly how the money will be used. Oh, there's someone by the front door that I need to talk to before she leaves. We'll talk about it over lunch—give me a call at the office.''

Gina nodded numbly.

She wanted to climb under the table and hide. Or better yet, she could just put her face into the punch bowl and drown.

But as the shock began to wear off, her mind started to work again. Just because the idea had been entirely her own didn't make it a bad one. Maybe it *was* sheer genius, as Anne had said—just look how many people seemed to agree.

Of course they're not the ones who would have to actually make it all work.

But that was defeatist thinking, and there was no room for anything of the sort if she was going to run a successful fund-raising campaign. Or for that matter a successful museum. Realism was one thing—pessimism another.

And giving up was impossible. She had already gone much too far down the road to admit that the whole thing had been a misunderstanding. She would look like a fool, but—much worse—if the museum's director lost her credibility, so did the institution.

Abruptly, Gina realized that while she'd been standing there thinking, the majority of the guests had departed. The noise level had dropped by at least half, and the waiters who had circulated all evening with trays of drinks and canapés were now gathering up empty glasses and used plates.

She found Anne Garrett still at the front door, dispensing hugs and goodbyes.

"Is there a phone I can use to call a cab?" Gina asked.

"Of course," Anne said. "But if you want my advice…"

"Only if you're willing to put it in writing," Gina said, not quite under her breath.

Anne laughed. "I'd suggest that you get to know your adversary. Dez!"

Gina hadn't seen him till then, leaning against a doorway leading into a big dining room, with his back to the entrance hall. He turned without haste, and she looked past him to see that he'd been talking to Jennifer Carleton.

"Dez, Gina needs a ride," Anne said, and as if the matter was settled she turned her attention to the next group of departing guests.

"Going my way?" Dez asked lazily.

Gina looked beyond him to where Jennifer was waiting. "Only if you're headed for your office, I expect."

"I wasn't actually planning to go back to work tonight. Unless of course you and Anne have come up with a new twist to this whole conspiracy so I have no other choice."

"Not at all. I just meant I'd hate to trouble you if you've already made plans."

Anne turned her head. "So polite," she mocked. "Knock it off, both of you, and get out of here."

Dez clicked his heels together, saluted Anne, and offered his arm to Gina. Rather than make a fuss, she took it. But as soon as they had left the house and were far enough down the sidewalk to be outside the circle of light where they could still be easily observed from inside, she stopped. "I'm serious," she said. "I don't want to put you to any trouble. So if Jennifer was expecting you to drive her home—"

"Then Jennifer would have been disappointed in any case."

"You could just call a cab for me."

Dez tossed his keys to the valet and looked her over thoughtfully. "I'm not planning to bury your mutilated body in the sand on Nicolet Point, you know."

"That's a comfort," Gina muttered.

"Not that I wouldn't like to," he went on as if she hadn't spoken. "But Anne knows you left with me, and I'd hate to have my name splashed all over the front page of the *Chronicle* as a suspect. It would not be good for my reputation."

"I thought you didn't care about your reputation."

"I didn't think I did either," he said earnestly. "But thanks to you, I've realized how much my good name means to me."

"But only when it comes to being suspected of murder."

"That's pretty much where I draw the line, yes."

Gina laughed. "All right. If you really don't mind giving me a ride… I suppose in a way I'm doing you a favor."

The valet returned with a sleek little sports car—dark green, Gina thought, though it was always hard to tell under streetlights what color something really was.

Dez helped her in and walked around to slide behind the wheel. "Doing me a favor how?" He sounded wary, Gina thought.

"At least Jennifer had to stop wheedling at you about the Carousel Ball."

"She wasn't wheedling."

"Then she's changed." Gina bit her tongue an instant too late. "Sorry—I shouldn't have said that." *Even if it's true*.

"Oh, she tried coaxing for a while. Then she switched to guilt. I expect nagging would have been next. She just hasn't figured out yet that manipulation isn't going to change my mind."

"Somehow," Gina mused, "I feel there's a message for me hidden in there."

"You have good instincts, my dear. Where are we going, besides toward my office?"

"A couple of blocks beyond the museum, on Belmont Street. So the Carousel Ball won't be held at Tyler-Royale? The dance isn't till November, I know, but that's only a few months off."

"In the property business, a few months can be forever."

"So that must mean you've made up your mind, if you're planning to be knocking down the building by November. What have you decided to build there?"

He shot a glance at her. "You sound awfully calm about the idea all of a sudden."

Gina shrugged. "Well, you do keep pointing out that it's none of my business what you do with your building."

"I wish I believed the message was actually sinking in. I'm not going to tell you, you know."

"Why not? Carla's already filled me in on all the gossip and speculation. Wouldn't it be better if you told me yourself, so I'd be sure to have it right?"

He was looking at her as if she'd lost her mind.

Apparently not, Gina thought. "Surely you're not ashamed of your plan…so what can it possibly be, for you to need to keep it such a secret?"

"What did Carla tell you?"

He sounded only vaguely interested, but Gina wasn't fooled. "Why should I give you the satisfaction of knowing what she said?"

"Because maybe you'll be able to guess the truth from my reactions, if you get anywhere close."

"That might actually be entertaining," Gina conceded. "All right. She says the talk around town is— How long did you date her, anyway?"

"Carla?"

Gina nodded firmly. "Don't try to deny it. Some things are obvious."

Dez shook his head as if it hurt, but he answered promptly enough. "Once. If you can even call it a date—which I wouldn't, myself."

"Only once? So that's why she's not exactly neutral when she talks about you. What did you do? Take her hiking through a mosquito-laden marsh? Or—I know. You just never called her back afterward."

"I was manipulated into escorting her to the Carousel Ball last year."

"I thought you told me you couldn't be manipulated," Gina said gently. "But never mind trying to explain that. Carla says the talk is that you're thinking of adding an apartment tower and a shopping mall to your empire."

"Hey, next time you see Carla, pass on my thanks for the idea. I'll look into it."

"You expect me to believe you haven't already? In any case, I don't believe she's right."

He shot her a quizzical look.

"Oh, the apartment tower, maybe. But the shopping mall?" Gina shook her head. "If a wide-spectrum department store like Tyler-Royale couldn't survive in that location, a mall doesn't stand a chance."

"Ah. You forget all the people who'll be living in the apartments. They have to buy their bologna and cheese somewhere."

"And after paying their rent, that's about all they'll be able to afford, I expect. I still don't think that's what you're planning, or you'd have dodged the question with more finesse. Turn right at the corner. I live in one of the row houses—the third one down on the west side of the street. Thanks for the ride, by the way."

He pulled the car in to the curb. "Aren't you going to invite me in for coffee?"

"There would be no point in it," Gina said earnestly. "I don't keep hazelnut on hand."

"I'd just like to see what the place looks like inside. These used to be pretty stylish—back in the days when Essie's house was a mansion."

"Essie's house is still a mansion."

"Not if you do everything to it that Jim Conklin says you're planning to do."

The trouble, Gina thought, was that Jim Conklin might have said almost anything at all, true or not. And Dez's voice had held a note of warning…

"On second thought," she said, "would you like to come in for a cup of coffee?"

"I'd love some." He killed the engine. "I thought you'd never ask."

Gina led the way upstairs. Under her slight weight, the squeaky stair protested only feebly, but when Dez hit it, the creak brought a rustle from the downstairs apartment. The door opened a crack and an eye peered out at them.

"Hello, Mrs. Mason," Gina said pleasantly.

The woman sniffed and closed her door.

"Nice neighbors," Dez murmured. "Or do you make a habit of bringing men home for her to check out? And if so, how do you think I scored on her scale?"

Gina ignored him.

Though she'd always liked the high ceilings and big windows, tonight her apartment felt smaller and the air more stuffy than it ever had before. Though perhaps, she thought, that was simply due to the presence of one large male. Dez wasn't exactly pacing, but he looked as if he'd like to.

She kept one eye on him as she made coffee—extra strong and not decaffeinated, because it wasn't her problem if he didn't get any sleep at all. He seemed, she thought, to be memorizing the place.

"There's one thing that still puzzles me," he said finally.

Gina kept her voice light. "Only one?"

"Well, maybe two, now that you mention it. Or three. Why is it such a big secret that you're planning to build onto Essie's house?"

"I wouldn't call it a big secret." She got a mug down from the cabinet.

Dez shook his head. "I stay pretty much on top of what's going on in Lakemont, and I hadn't heard a word about that till tonight. No architects' gossip, no engineers' talk. Nothing."

"Oh, that's easy to explain. You haven't heard any speculation from architects or engineers because we haven't consulted any." She watched him from the corner of her eye. Was he really turning slightly green?

At any rate, Gina thought philosophically, now she'd experienced life's ultimate thrill. Striking Dez Kerrigan speechless—nothing else she ever did could possibly top that.

She took pity on him. "It was only an idea, not a plan. We hadn't consulted experts yet because we were only beginning to think about additions when the Tyler-Royale building became a possibility."

"It's not a possibility," Dez said flatly.

"Well, not if you insist on knocking it down. But do you seriously believe enough people want to live downtown to make an apartment tower profitable?"

He didn't answer. Gina poured his coffee, and when she finally looked up at him, holding out the cup, she realized he wasn't simply pretending not to have heard the question. He was scraping one index finger along the other in a gesture that released a well of emotion from Gina's earliest memories. "Shame on you," he said gently. "I thought you'd didn't believe Carla's conclusions."

She had to pull herself back. *Oh, yes—Carla and the apartment tower.*

Dez took the mug. "So you've been planning to add chunks to Essie's house even though you haven't a clue whether it's possible, much less wise."

"Of course it's possible—I know that much about buildings and codes. If you have enough money, you could add a museum wing to an airplane. And in that neighborhood we can build right up to the property line without special permits."

"That fact alone should make you stop and think."

"Why?"

"Because if you can, so can your neighbors."

Gina thought about it, and shrugged. "I don't see that it makes much difference. We're not going to, and neither are they."

"They must all be nice and cooperative people," Dez mused. "Sort of like the woman who lives downstairs."

"Well, as far as Mrs. Mason is concerned," Gina admitted, "I'd appreciate it, when you leave, if you'd make sure to step on that squeaky stair again."

"Just so it's obvious that I'm actually going? Make it worth my while, and I'll jump up and down on it."

"That won't be necessary. Why should it bother you, anyway, no matter what we do to the museum? Essie's house has nothing to do with you." But the words seemed to echo inside Gina's head, as if there was some extra meaning that she was missing. She frowned a little, but before she could think about it Dez had gone on.

"The other thing that puzzles me," he said, "is that you're willing to sell Essie's house at all. You seem to feel reverence for everything Essie owned, and yet you're willing to hand over her house to the highest bidder no matter what they intend to do with it.''

"That's just not true, Dez. I'll be very careful about who ends up with it. And it'll be far better for the house to be a home again than to be chopped up as we'd have to do to turn it into galleries.''

"But you *can't* be careful,'' Dez said flatly. "For one thing, it's not your decision—it's your board's, and they're going to want every last dollar it'll bring.''

Gina bit her lip in consternation. He was probably right about that. They'd *need* every last dollar.

"And you aren't going to convince me that Jim Conklin will worry himself out of sleeping at night because he's afraid Essie's house isn't in safe hands.'' He drained his coffee cup. "Mind if I pour myself another one?''

Gina was too annoyed with herself to do anything but wave a hand vaguely toward the coffeemaker. How had she managed to avoid allowing herself to see the obvious, when it had been so clear to Dez?

Because you didn't want to think about the reality, that's why.

Essie's house wasn't likely to bring much money, under any circumstances. But the board, faced with putting a different building into shape to house the museum, would want to squeeze every cent they could out of the property they were selling. She couldn't blame them for that—it was the only sensible thing to do. Besides, it was a matter of public trust. They couldn't honestly ask the public for donations to pay for a new museum while at the same time they were giving away the assets they already possessed.

And there was yet another hitch in her rose-colored plan, now that she stopped to think about it. The very people who should have the house—a young family who had energy to spare to make it beautiful again—would likely not be in a position to pay much for it. And if they did put in a sizable bid, they wouldn't have cash left to do the necessary restorations...

Talk about being hooked on a dilemma.

She said, "We'll worry about that when the time comes."

"Very sensible," Dez agreed.

That surprised her, and she shot an inquisitive look at him.

"Because the time won't come unless you find some other building you like better," he explained. "And as long as you have your heart set on Tyler-Royale, anybody who's waiting for this house might as well try to buy the lake."

Gina refused to rise to the bait. She pretended to ignore him and started to clean the coffeemaker, dumping the rest of the brew down the drain. The hot, bitter smell almost choked her. How could he drink the stuff, anyway?

"I guess this means I'm not having a third cup," Dez murmured. "There's one more thing I'd like to know, too. What was it that made Essie so special to you? As far as I could see, she was a very boring old woman."

"Perhaps," Gina said sweetly, "you only thought so because you were a boring kid at the time you made that assessment."

"Ouch. All right, I deserved that one. But you must have been about the same age when you decided she was interesting. At least you said you'd been hanging around here for ten or twelve years before she died. So how old were you?"

"I was thirteen," Gina said. She didn't look at him.

"That must have been about the same time you were in school with Jennifer Carleton."

What had Jennifer told him? "Somewhere around then, I guess."

"So what caused your fascination with Essie?"

I wonder what you'd think if I told you. "I suppose you could call it hero-worship."

He moved closer. "For *Essie?* You're joking. But it has to have been more than just being interested in her old stuff."

"Not really." Gina ruefully concluded that if she scrubbed the coffeemaker any longer, she'd likely clean a hole straight through the glass. So she set the carafe aside and put down her brush. "It started out as a job. The first task was to take inventory of her collection."

"She let a thirteen-year-old kid handle everything she owned?"

"Under supervision."

"I'll bet. She must have hovered over you like a surveillance drone."

"And as I worked with her and listened to her stories—"

"Speaking of drones…"

"She wasn't monotonous or dreary at all. I should have thought you'd be particularly interested in everything she had to say, since most of it was about the early days of Kerrigan County and about your ancestors. How much do you know about Desmond Kerrigan, anyway?"

"The question isn't how much I know," Dez countered. "It's how much I want to know—which isn't much at all. So you worked for her, and you got in the habit of listening to her stories…"

"I got in the habit of appreciating history," Gina corrected.

"So you're saying Essie was the making of you."

In more ways than you would believe. "She certainly changed the course of my life."

He was silent. The only sound was the click of his empty coffee cup as he set it on the counter beside her.

Gina rinsed out the sink and dried her hands. Finally, wary of the long pause, she turned to face him. He was standing closer than she'd realized.

"Thank you," Dez said soberly.

Gina shrugged. "I can make better coffee than that, when I'm not in a rush."

"I didn't mean the coffee. Thank you for befriending an old woman who shouldn't have been so alone."

She felt her jaw go slack, and she had trouble getting a breath. Was it actually regret she was hearing in his voice? "I can see why the stories would seem boring to you," she managed finally. "But they were all new to me, and that made them exciting."

He smiled a little. "You must have been very special to her."

And just how, Gina thought, was she supposed to respond to that?

But Dez didn't seem to expect an answer. He looked down at her for a long moment, and then under his breath he said, "Oh, to heck with it." He cupped her chin in his hand and turned her face up, and kissed her.

His mouth moved slowly and gently against hers, as lightly as if her lips might bruise under pressure. Too stunned to respond, Gina stood as still as if she were frozen. But inside she was awash in warmth and confusion. He wasn't even touching her, except for the tips of his fingers resting in the hollow just under the point of her chin, but she felt as if every inch of her had been caressed with sandpaper. Every nerve was quivering.

When he raised his head, she had to make an effort to keep her voice level. "And that was your way of saying thank you for what I meant to Essie, I suppose."

He lifted an eyebrow. "Of course."

"I'm glad we have that clear." She stepped aside. "Good night, Dez."

He didn't move. "The next one won't be. It'll be a lesson in how to kiss."

"I don't need lessons, thank you."

"Yes, you do. Let me know when you're ready to move on."

Before she could find her voice, he was gone. As she moved to lock the door behind him, she heard the telltale step near the bottom of the staircase creak under his weight.

So she'd been wrong about Dez Kerrigan—he *did* have a sentimental bone in his body. She wouldn't bet on there being more than one, of course. But at least he had finally realized how much he had missed by not getting to know Essie.

Essie—who was really not much like the somber, strait-laced schoolmarm that she had pretended to be. She'd scared Gina half to death, that first day…so long ago now that it felt as if it had happened in another world, another life. To another person.

Because I was a different person back then, Gina thought. And that change was entirely thanks to Essie.

Kissing lessons, indeed. Though it hadn't been a bad recovery, Gina had to admit. What a way for the man to cover up a rare moment of uncontrolled sentiment—by teasing her with the threat of kissing lessons.

No doubt he thought she'd be so excited at the prospect that she'd forget all about him getting just a bit maudlin over Essie. But then he didn't know Gina as well as he thought. She wasn't distracted.

Not in the least.

CHAPTER SIX

GINA took one long last look around what had once been Essie Kerrigan's dining room. Now it was the museum's conference and meeting room, and on Monday evening the table was set up for the regular meeting of the board of directors. Eight chairs were arranged precisely, and Gina's most regular and reliable volunteer was giving the long mahogany table a last-minute polishing. Gina followed along, putting out notepads and pencils at each seat. Coffee was perking in a big old pot on the sideboard, and a tray of soft drinks sat nearby.

"I think the only thing we still need is the water pitchers," Gina said. "If you'll bring those in, Eleanor, I'll get the glasses. I really appreciate you coming in to help me set up. Especially on a day when you weren't scheduled to work in the first place."

Eleanor shrugged. "It's not that I don't like the visitors, but I always enjoy being here on a day when the museum's closed. It's fun to pretend—" She broke off with a grin. "Besides, my husband's taking the kids fishing tonight, and I'd do anything rather than go along."

Gina laughed. "In that case, before you bring in the water pitchers, will you run up and get the copies of the agenda off my desk? I just realized I forgot to bring them down. Then you can go, if you like—if you're sure the coast will be clear at home."

"Actually," Eleanor said, "I was thinking of staying to listen. I mean—usually nobody shows up for the board

Play the Lucky Hearts Game

and get...

2 FREE BOOKS
and a **FREE MYSTERY GIFT**...

YOURS to KEEP!

yes! I have scratched off the silver card. Please send me my *2 FREE BOOKS* and *FREE mystery GIFT*. I understand that I am under no obligation to purchase any books as explained on the back of this card.

Scratch Here!

then look below to see what your cards get you... 2 Free Books & a Free Mystery Gift!

386 HDL DU6V　　　　　**186 HDL DU7D**

FIRST NAME　　　　　　　LAST NAME

ADDRESS

APT.#　　　　CITY

STATE/PROV.　　　ZIP/POSTAL CODE　　　(H-R-08/03)

Twenty-one gets you
2 FREE BOOKS
and a **FREE MYSTERY GIFT!**

Twenty gets you
2 FREE BOOKS!

Nineteen gets you
1 FREE BOOK!

TRY AGAIN!

Offer limited to one per household and not valid to current Harlequin Romance® subscribers. All orders subject to approval.

© 2002 HARLEQUIN ENTERPRISES LTD.
® and TM are trademarks owned by Harlequin Enterprises Ltd.

► DETACH AND MAIL CARD TODAY! ►

The Harlequin Reader Service® — Here's how it works:

BUSINESS REPLY MAIL
FIRST-CLASS MAIL   PERMIT NO. 717-003   BUFFALO, NY

POSTAGE WILL BE PAID BY ADDRESSEE

HARLEQUIN READER SERVICE
3010 WALDEN AVE
PO BOX 1867
BUFFALO NY 14240-9952

NO POSTAGE
NECESSARY
IF MAILED
IN THE
UNITED STATES

meetings except for the members. But that doesn't mean that nobody else is allowed to come, does it?''

Gina was startled. ''Of course you can stay. Since we get part of our funding from the taxpayers of Kerrigan County, our board meetings are public and anyone can attend. But—'' She hesitated. ''Is there something going on that I should know about? Do you have a problem?''

''Who, me? Of course not.'' Eleanor looked down at the floor. ''I'm just wondering what the board's planning to do about the house. If they're going to get this big new building, are they going to sell the house?''

Was there a strange sort of quaver in the woman's voice? ''Eleanor, I know you love this house. But I wouldn't get too worried just yet.''

''I'm not worried, exactly. Oh, it's silly of me—because I know even if it was for sale my husband and I couldn't afford it. We couldn't stretch the budget that far. So it's probably just as well.'' She gave a final swipe to the table and tucked her cleaning cloth into her belt.

''In any case, the board won't make any final decisions tonight,'' Gina said. ''But I'll keep in mind what you said.''

''For what it's worth,'' Eleanor said a bit glumly. She hurried off toward the stairs.

The side door by the porte cochere creaked open, and Gina gave a nervous little shiver and went to greet the first arrival. To her relief, it was the president of the historical society. She'd been hoping to have a private word with him before the rest of the board members arrived.

He looked down his Roman nose at her and said, ''I hope you can explain what's been going on.''

''I'll certainly try, sir. I'm glad you're early tonight— I've been trying to reach you all weekend. You must have been out of town.''

He nodded. ''My daughter had her baby, so my wife

insisted that we go to Minneapolis to be with her. It's her third child and our fifth grandchild—you'd think everybody would be a little calmer about the whole reproductive process by now. But no, my wife had to be there to hold our daughter's hand through the whole thing.''

Sounds pretty wonderful to me. But Gina bit her lip—it wasn't her place to comment. Instead, she said, ''I'm sorry not to have warned you, but I had no idea that reporter would call you about the Tyler-Royale building.''

''Odd thing, wasn't it? Of course it's a shame that Kerrigan's going to knock it down.''

''I don't think we should give up quite so soon, sir.''

''Oh, we'll do what we can. But obviously you haven't gone up against him before. I have, a time or two.''

And the buildings are gone. He didn't need to say the words, because Gina could hear them in the tone of his voice. Matter-of-fact, calm, resigned.

''In any case,'' he went on, ''even if it was given to us on a platter, we couldn't use all that space.''

''That's something I wanted to discuss with the board tonight, sir. I think there is a practical way to use the entire building. You see—''

But before she could go on, the door opened again, and within a few minutes the entire board had assembled and were milling around the dining room, pouring coffee and catching up on news.

The last to arrive was Jim Conklin, with a stranger in tow. He brought the man straight to Gina. ''This is the expert I was telling you about,'' he said. ''Nathan Haynes—he's an architect with a firm here in town. I've talked to him about the expansion plans, and he's going to take a look and give us some suggestions.''

The board president tapped on the table. ''Let's get started, now that everyone's here.''

Chairs scraped against the oak floor. Gina took her regular seat at the foot of the table; Eleanor had brought in an extra chair and sat nearby, a short distance away from the table.

The rustle died as everyone settled down. The president said, "The meeting is called—"

The side door creaked as it opened.

Who could that be? Gina wondered. Nobody was missing, nobody was late. They were expecting no guests tonight.

Her heart was beating faster than usual as she considered the possibilities. A visitor, perhaps; while the hours were clearly posted, all the traffic might have led someone to believe the museum was open tonight. Or…someone with a very different agenda. Like robbery.

Darn Dez Kerrigan, she thought. All his propaganda about the neighborhood being so unsafe was beginning to take its toll on her—she was actually wishing she'd sent Eleanor to lock the door after the last board member had arrived. Never before, in all the time she'd worked at the museum, had such a thought come into her head.

Then, as if her random thought had called him up like a ghost at a séance, Dez appeared in the doorway. "Hello, everybody," he said. "Sorry to be late, but I ended up walking over from my office because I couldn't find a place to park."

Gina's heart rate didn't slow. *In the long run, I might have preferred the robber.*

"You know," he went on easily, "you really ought to consider that problem before you decide to make this place even bigger." He looked around the room and his gaze came to rest on Gina. "Where will I find an extra chair, Gina? Or shall I just perch on the arm of yours?"

* * *

The shock in Gina's face was priceless, even though Dez was a bit surprised that she'd reacted at all. Had she really not anticipated that he would show up tonight?

She actually seemed to be turning slightly blue, as if she'd stopped breathing. He considered the options. The Heimlich maneuver probably wouldn't do much good since it wasn't food she'd choked on, but his mere presence. That seemed to leave him with a choice—toss a glass of water in her face, or bend her over his arm and kiss her. Either would probably do the trick as far as shocking her back to reality, but there was no question which method he would prefer. He wondered how she'd cast her vote.

Before he could act, however, Gina had pulled herself together. "Chairs are in the next room," she said. Her voice was a little lower than usual, and a little less steady, but otherwise she was back to normal. The others at the table might not even have noticed.

Dez awarded her points for a quick comeback and went to get a chair. When he came back, he set it down right next to hers, though he studiously avoided meeting her eyes. Instead, he was surveying the board members. He nodded to the president—a nice enough guy, even if he did have some strange notions about old buildings—and to Jim Conklin. And next to Jim... "Hi, Nate," he said to the architect. "What are you doing here?"

Nathan Haynes grinned. "Pretty much the same thing you are, I expect," he said. "Just observing things at the moment."

That was odd, Dez thought as he settled into his chair. An architect without a plan? Besides, Gina had told him they hadn't hired either an architect or an engineer yet.... His memory twinged. This must be the expert Jim Conklin had been referring to, at that infernal cocktail party—the one he said he'd gone to so much trouble to persuade to come to this gathering.

The chairman called the meeting to order and the secretary began to read the minutes.

Dez reached over Gina's shoulder and picked up her copy of the evening's agenda. *Possible cooperation with other organizations to form a museum center.* Nothing surprising about that one. *Fund-raising events*—it should be an interesting evening.

Beside him, Gina shifted in her chair and toyed with a pencil. He watched from the corner of his eye, trying to gauge the precise moment when she wouldn't be able to stand it any more.

She held out longer than he expected. But as the secretary droned on, she leaned toward him and said under her breath, "What are you doing here?"

"Being a good citizen," he whispered back. "Keeping an eye on how my tax money is being spent."

She gave a cute little snort and turned her attention back to the discussion. Or at least she pretended to focus on the board.

Dez leaned back in his chair, folded his arms, and settled in to enjoy himself.

Gina had half expected that when the meeting ended, Dez would be the first one out the door. Instead, he drifted off to the corner of the room where Jim Conklin and his architect friend were talking to the board president. As she unplugged the still-hot coffeepot, she heard the architect say, "Hey, Dez, is it true that you're going to consolidate the whole red-light district under one roof in the Tyler-Royale building? I heard at City Hall that the mayor's thinking of giving you an award for public service for cleaning up the town."

Gina wasn't a bit surprised when Dez only grunted and swiftly volunteered to carry the coffeepot into the kitchen for her.

By the time she and Eleanor had finished clearing away the mess in the dining room, the board members had all left and the house was quiet. Eleanor began to wash the dishes while Gina went to lock the door.

She found Dez standing in the silent hallway, one hand on the newel post at the base of the long curving staircase, looking up into the dimness at the top.

"I'm surprised you're still hanging around," she said. "Especially considering that you didn't have a word to say the whole way through the meeting. If you weren't going to put your two cents' worth into the discussion, why did you bother to come?"

"If I'd had anything to say, I'd have said it. But I thought you were doing such a fine job that there was nothing to add."

He sounded so innocent that Gina shot a suspicious look at him. "Your halo is a little askew," she pointed out. "The truth is, if the board had threatened to do anything that might interfere with your plans, you'd have had plenty to say."

"Well, in that case, of course, I'd have had to straighten them out."

"*Straighten them out?* Do you absolutely always believe that you're right? Never mind. I suppose I should be happy that at least you've stopped pretending to be just a private citizen checking up on how your taxes are being spent."

"But that's exactly what I am," Dez protested.

"Somehow I doubt you devote this much time and energy to every board and committee and organization that winds up with a few dollars of your money, Dez."

"That's true—but then some uses of my hard-earned

cash inspire deeper feelings in me than others do.'' He cast an appraising glance around the hallway. ''Like the whole idea of pouring it into modern wings attached to this house.''

Gina put her hands on her hips. ''You know, I wish you'd make up your mind what you want. Over the weekend you seemed to think we should stay put and build additions. Now you sound as if you think we shouldn't. Not that our decisions will rest on your advice, of course, but it would be nice if you'd stop playing hopscotch.''

''It would be a waste of money.''

''And this is a waste of breath. I already know what you're going to say—there's no sense in building on because we already have a shortage of parking. So what? Not every one of our visitors has a car. Maybe we'll start a downtown trolley line, or a shuttle bus service—something that would actually be a public service. Honestly, why you think it's any of your business—''

Dez was shaking his head. ''That's not what I mean. Gina, this place is falling down around your head and you can't even see it.''

The somber tone of his voice sent chills down Gina's spine, but only for a moment. Then she rolled her eyes and smiled. ''You don't expect me to take your word for that, surely. You're the king of demolition. Your entire philosophy is *If it's more than fifteen minutes old, dynamite it.* Which reminds me, what are you planning to do with Lakemont Tower when it starts creaking? Because, you know, it has a much shorter life expectancy than the warehouses you knocked down to build it.''

''Just remember that I tried to warn you,'' Dez said.

''I'll be sure to make a note of it. In any case, who says we're staying here? I thought my suggestion for turning the

Tyler-Royale building into a museum center went over very well with the board.''

"Or else they were too polite to tell you what they really thought of the idea.''

"It may take them a while to come around," Gina conceded. "But in the long run, they'll see that it makes perfect sense. Each museum could still be independent while sharing most of the expensive extras. There would be only one gift shop to stock and run. One security system. One receptionist and ticketing booth—''

"Have you actually talked to all the other museums?''

"Not every last one of them. Is that why you didn't plunge into the discussion? Because you thought I was bluffing? Or is it because you're confident I can't convince enough of the other organizations to make the plan work?''

"No. The reason I didn't plunge into the discussion was because there was no need. It doesn't matter if you get everybody on the west coast of Lake Michigan to agree. I'm still the one who owns the option.''

"That is a problem," Gina admitted. "Seriously, Dez— how much do you want for that option?''

"It's not for sale.''

"Come on. You can't expect me to believe that. You said yourself that where there was one deal there could always be another.''

"Not in this case.''

"You could build your apartment tower anywhere. You'll be tearing down St. Francis Church anyway, right? I mean, you're not planning to start up your own congregation there, are you?''

"I don't think leading a religious flock is quite my vocation.''

"And you're not going to renovate the church so you can live there?''

He didn't answer. But had he actually shuddered just a little at the notion? Gina wouldn't be surprised. If his idea of living space was anything like his office... Not that his office wasn't nice enough. In fact, it was so starkly simple that it had a quiet kind of elegance. But it was a whole world away from the age-frayed elegance of St. Francis Church.

She held out both hands, palms up. "So what's the problem? Put your tower there. Instead of being smack in the middle of downtown, it would be right on the edge. Instead of overwhelming the central city, it would complement it."

"The site's not large enough."

Gina shrugged. "Surely that's not enough to stop you. Just add a few more stories onto the top."

"That's much more easily said than done. When you're talking about living units—"

"Ah."

His eyes narrowed. "What do you mean, *Ah?*"

"You just admitted that despite all the denials, you *are* building an apartment tower. Wait till I tell Carla she was right."

Dez shook his head. "I was speaking hypothetically."

"Sure you were. And I moved here from Mars, too."

"Now *that* I could believe," he muttered.

Gina ignored him. "How much do you want for the option?"

"I didn't hear the board approving you to negotiate. So I'm not going to get into a pointless discussion."

"There must be something you want." Too late, she realized that what she'd said could have an infinite number of meanings, most of them off-color. "Of course, I don't mean—"

"I thought you said you were going to negotiate. Not that you have anything much to offer, since I also didn't hear the board authorizing any money for this deal. Unless you're thinking of things like getting in a hot tub with me— and though that would be interesting, it would hardly make financial sense.''

Gina decided to ignore that entire line of conversation and pretend that she wasn't turning ever-so-slightly pink. ''You wouldn't expect a board to speculate about how much money you might be willing to take when you're right there in the room, surely. And we do have resources.''

He ticked them off on his fingers. ''An annual allotment from Kerrigan County taxpayers. Sales of season tickets and museum memberships. Admissions fees for one-time visitors. The odd donation and memorial fund. Oh, and the proceeds from Essie's estate and life insurance. That's the one sizable chunk of cash the museum has, but of course it's tied up tight in trust with the income already budgeted—mostly to pay your salary.'' He must have seen surprise in her face, for his eyebrows raised a bit. ''I can do research too.''

''You overlooked the money we've already set aside for expansion and remodeling.''

''You mean your rainy-day fund? Sweetheart, believe me—there's thunder in the distance, and it's getting closer.'' He cast an appraising eye around the hallway once more.

''Are you admiring the paneling, or waiting for the ceiling to fall in?''

''Just noticing that the place does have its charms.'' He shot a sideways glance at her. ''Particularly when it's nearly dark inside. Whenever you decide for certain what you're going to do for a fund-raiser, by the way, let me know.'' He turned toward the door.

Gina stepped into his path. ''Why? So you can be sure to sabotage it?''

"Of course not, darling. So I can buy a ticket. You're going to need all the help you can get."

Before she could catch her breath, he was gone.

Eleanor had finished in the kitchen, and they went out together. Eleanor strolled down the driveway while Gina paused to get out her key. The lock was being unusually balky tonight, and it took her a couple of minutes to persuade it to work. But finally the house was secure and she walked down the drive to where Eleanor was standing, hands in the pockets of her jacket, staring back at the house.

"It's a grand old place," she said. "I didn't think so at first, when I started to work here. I thought it was spooky and musty and old and tired—sort of like Essie herself, as a matter of fact." She shot a sidelong look at Gina as if thinking she might have said too much. "But after a while... The house sort of creeps into your heart."

"Sort of like Essie did," Gina said softly.

"Yeah," Eleanor agreed. "Well—see you tomorrow." She turned the corner and walked down the street to where her car was parked.

Gina stood still for a moment longer, taking a long look at the house.

After a while, the house sort of creeps into your heart.

What was it Dez had said? *The place does have its charms.*

That was different, Gina thought. He'd been talking at random, changing the subject because he was unwilling even to talk about selling that option.

But why wouldn't he put a price on it? Not because he absolutely wouldn't consider selling, that was sure—because he'd said himself that he was always open to a deal.

Was it because he thought it wasn't worth the effort to decide on a figure? He seemed to think that whatever the price was, Gina would have trouble raising it—and that was true enough, she admitted.

Or was it because he wanted something other than money?

Was it possible that he wanted Essie's house?

You've been drinking way too much coffee, Gina told herself. *You've got a major case of the jitters, to even be thinking that way.*

But there was a basic contradiction in what he'd said. He'd told her that the house was falling down, but he'd also said he was beginning to notice its good points. And then he'd quickly changed the subject to fund-raising.

Very quickly.

This place does have its charms. She'd bet any amount of money that he'd never said anything of the sort about any other old building. Only this one.

But Essie's house was different from all the other old buildings he'd ever dealt with. It was his great-grandfather who had built it. It was his family heritage that seeped from every brick.

Was it possible that despite his long lack of interest Dez had begun to care about those things? He'd asked a lot of questions—for Dez, at least—about Essie. He'd seemed to regret missing out on knowing her. And he'd spent a couple of hours wandering around the house the night he'd first visited the museum. What was it that he had found so fascinating? The exhibits showing historical Kerrigan County? Or the building that housed them?

Gina knew he was capable of sentiment, because he'd proved it the night he'd taken her home after Anne Garrett's cocktail party. He'd kissed her in a sort of sudden rush of gratitude that she'd been there for Essie in his aunt's final years.

And if she had to stake next month's rent on the question

of why he'd come to the meeting tonight, she would bet that it was for much the same reason that Eleanor had. To find out first-hand what was going to happen to the house. Even if he didn't want to admit it, he cared.

Maybe, Gina thought, there was a deal to be made here after all.

Dez sat back in his chair and surveyed the man sitting across the conference table from him. Nathan Haynes finished jotting notes in a pocket calendar, looked once more at the rough sketches Dez had handed him, and said, "I'll get to this as soon as I can, but it may be a while before I can do the actual drawings."

"Preliminaries are good enough. Just tell me whether we can do it." Dez flipped his notebook closed and asked casually, "Have you had a chance to look at the museum building yet?"

"Not in any detail. I was there this morning, as a matter of fact, but I was only getting started when you called."

"What are you going to advise they do?"

Nathan shook his head. "Dez, you know better than to think I'll discuss a client's business with another client. Or with anyone else for that matter, so don't ask an old girlfriend to call and quiz me, either."

Dez shrugged. "It was worth a try." He pushed his chair back. "Let me know when you have a tower to show me." He walked Nathan out to the parking lot, and when he came back he stopped beside his secretary's desk. "Did anything exciting happen while I was tied up?"

"Only a lunch invitation." The secretary moved a folder from one stack to another and looked up at him with a gleam of curiosity. "From Gina Haskell."

Now what is the woman up to? "I hope you told her I was busy."

"I told her you were in conference. She said she'd wait for you at The Maple Tree till one o'clock, just in case you could come."

"If she's lucky, she took a good book with her—because that's all the company she's going to have." Dez went back into his office. He tidied up the scraps of paper he and Nate had been pushing back and forth, putting them away so no chance visitor would get a glimpse, and sat down at his desk.

The woman had a nerve, expecting him to drop everything and rush off to have lunch with her. Though from what his secretary had said, perhaps she hadn't exactly *expected* it. Sarah had made it sound more like a hopeful invitation than a summons.

So what did Gina want to talk to him about? What had come up in the day and a half since the board meeting?

Nate said he hadn't looked at the museum in detail yet. But if he'd been there this morning... Had Nate already made a preliminary report? And if so, what had he told Gina?

Dez tossed his fountain pen down on the blotter and strode across his office. "I'm going out for lunch, Sarah."

The secretary didn't look up. "Cutting it a little close, aren't you?"

Dez fixed her with a stare. "I didn't say I was going to The Maple Tree."

"Of course not, sir. Shall I call to tell her you're on the way?"

Dez called over his shoulder, "Not if you still want to have a job this afternoon."

Sarah only grinned at him.

It was five minutes to one when he walked into The Maple Tree, and Gina was sitting at the bar. She was wearing something yellow—he noticed it mainly because it made her hair look even more like flame—and though she didn't have a book, she looked as if she'd like one. She was sitting very upright and looking straight ahead, and quite obviously she was trying to ignore the man on the next stool who was attempting to strike up a conversation.

Dez stood for a moment at the opposite side of the dining room, enjoying the sight. Then, without haste, he crossed the room.

"Sorry to be late, darling," he murmured. "Meetings can be such a pain." He cupped her chin in his palm and kissed her, slowly and thoroughly. She tasted of ginger ale and uncertainty. As he raised his head, he said, "What a surprise. The guy who was hitting on you just a minute ago seems to have been suddenly called away."

Gina's voice was husky. "I invited you for lunch, not..."

"A kissing lesson?" He felt just a little gruff himself. "That was just assignment one—how to kiss in public places in order to avoid men who want to accost you."

"I'm having a little trouble with the logic there, Dez. He may have wanted to accost me, but you actually did it."

"I'm sure you'll eventually work it out to your satisfaction. Is Bruce saving us a table?" He waved the maître d' over, and a moment later was holding a chair for Gina. "So why did you call this meeting?"

"You did tell me to let you know when I'd decided on a fund-raiser."

That was true, but Dez would give pretty good odds that wasn't the real reason they were here. "Oh, yes," he mused as he looked over the menu. "I've been giving thought to your fund-raising problems."

"I'll just bet you have. We've decided to hold an old-fashioned village fair on the lawn to kick off the campaign."

"Is that all? I'm disappointed. Still, keep the first ticket for me."

"I'll call Carla and have her bring a camera crew to show you buying it."

"You're too kind." He put the menu down, told the waiter to bring him a cup of coffee, and braced his elbows on the edge of the table. "Now, Gina my dear, you can tell me what this lunch is really about."

She looked down. "Well....I have a sort of proposition."

Dez thought about it and shook his head. "I'll listen, but unless this proposition involves a hot tub I don't think I'm going to be interested."

"What is it with you and hot tubs? Of course, this is only a preliminary offer because it would require board approval, but—"

His coffee arrived, along with another glass of ginger ale for Gina. He picked up his cup, inhaled the fragrance of hazelnut, and gestured for her to continue.

"I'm offering you a trade," she said. "Even up—Essie's house for your option to buy the Tyler-Royale building."

He choked on a mouthful of hot coffee. If she'd been trying to kill him, he thought, her timing couldn't have been better. It took a minute to stop coughing, and even then he was hoarse and could hardly get a full breath. "You want to trade *what?*"

She seemed a bit impatient at having to explain. "You give the museum your option to buy the building, and we give you Essie's house."

"That's what you call an even trade? No, Gina—I will not trade the Tyler-Royale building for Essie's house."

"I'm not asking for the whole *building,*" she said impatiently. "Just the *option.*"

"Offer me Essie's house and half a million dollars and I might think about it."

A look of cool calculation came into her eyes. "Half a million? Then I guess I'll just have to work harder at fund-raising."

"I said I *might* think about it," Dez warned.

She obviously wasn't listening. "Or perhaps I just need to get more creative...." She squared her shoulders and looked straight at him. "All right, Dez. How much is it worth for me to get into a hot tub with you?"

CHAPTER SEVEN

THE woman *was* trying to kill him, Dez decided. She hadn't managed to choke him to death with coffee, so she'd opted to try stopping his heart with astonishment.

"How much is it worth to you?" she repeated. "Because for—say—ten thousand dollars, I'd consider it."

"Ten *thousand*—" He cleared his throat and tried again. "You have an inflated idea of what an evening of your time is worth."

He could almost hear ice cubes tinkling in her voice. "And let's make it quite clear that my time is absolutely all I'm talking about."

"No hanky-panky in the hot tub," he agreed smoothly.

"And the ten thousand is payable to the museum fund. A cashier's check would do nicely."

I'll bet it would. "Incredibly selfless of you, Gina—to make such a sacrifice for the museum."

Her eyes had narrowed. "You don't think I'd do this for any other reason, do you?"

Mischief reared its head, and Dez tried without much success to bite back a grin. "Maybe not the first time. But once you've experienced the pleasures—" The expression in her eyes warned him not to push her any further, so he added hastily, "Give me a chance to think it over. I'll let you know." He pushed back his chair. "Thanks for the coffee. Sorry I can't stay for lunch."

Believe me, sweetheart, I'll let you know.

But it wasn't the hot tub he was thinking about as he

left The Maple Tree. It was her other off-the-wall suggestion that was nagging at him.

What on earth had she been thinking?

It was enough of an insult to suggest that he might consider trading his option to buy a square block of downtown
Lakemont for Essie Kerrigan's house. But then she'd offered to make it an even trade—and she'd sounded as if
she expected him to jump at the opportunity. No, it was
even more than that. She'd sounded as if she honestly
thought she was giving him a steal—that Essie's house was
a bargain at the price.

The woman was nuts. Or else she thought *he* was.

Dez was pulling out his cell phone and hitting speed-dial
as he strode to his car. When Nathan Haynes answered, he
sounded a bit breathless, and Dez grinned. "Sorry to interrupt you, Nate. Give the lady my apologies."

"This is no lady," Nate said. "Just a big outcropping of
rock that didn't show up on the preliminary surveys. The
excavators hit it while they were digging the trenches for
a foundation and we're either going to have to take it out
the hard way or redesign the building."

"As long as it's not one of my projects—"

"I couldn't be that lucky. And if you're calling about
your drawings, no, I haven't got them done yet. I know it's
been an entire hour since I left your office, but—"

"That's not why I'm calling. Did you talk to Gina
Haskell this morning at the museum?"

"Dez, you know I can't tell you that."

"I'm not asking what you discussed—just whether you
talked to her."

"I wouldn't call it talking." Nate sounded cautious. "I
said good morning and so did she."

Dez frowned. "But that's all?"

"Pretty much. Why?"

"Nothing." Maybe Gina wasn't quite as crazy as he'd thought. "Nate, don't be in a hurry to do those drawings of mine."

"Oh, that's a bonus. What you mean is, you won't bug me about them till tomorrow."

"No," Dez said soberly. "What I mean is that I may—just may—want to make some fundamental changes in the plan. I'll let you know."

Well, that entire scheme had gone flat as a pancake, Gina thought philosophically. But she'd succeeded in providing Dez Kerrigan with his day's entertainment—at least, his eyes had turned a more brilliant green than she'd ever seen them before.

Of course, being amused hadn't made the man let down his guard even an iota. He hadn't missed a beat. *Essie's house and half a million dollars and I might think about it.*

Not that he would actually hold out for that much, or expect it. Negotiations always started with outlandish figures; it was part of the game. She had expected that Dez would want something extra thrown in to sweeten the pot.

But at least—finally—he'd stopped saying the option wasn't for sale and he'd actually set a price on it. No matter how preposterous the figure was, he'd started to deal, and now he couldn't back out. By putting a figure on the table he had, in effect, agreed to sell.

If they could reach a mutually satisfactory price.

So how much money would he insist on getting? She'd been hoping that he'd take a hundred thousand dollars. It was less than he'd paid for the option, that was true. But by the time everything was figured in, he would still be buying the Kerrigan mansion for a song.

Now it didn't seem likely that Dez would be quite that flexible.

It would be reasonable, however, to think that he'd asked for at least twice what he expected to settle for. So at tops, a quarter of a million should satisfy him. And in fact, that would not only give him a bonus over what he'd paid, but it was easy money—all he'd had to do to earn it was to own the option for a week or two.

He could use the leftover fifty grand to redecorate Essie's house to his taste.

Gina wrinkled her nose at the thought of Essie's house swathed in slate-gray carpet and drapes like those in his office. But at least she wouldn't have to see it. And though Essie might not have appreciated the decor, Gina was certain she wouldn't have made a fuss about it, either. She would have been happy to see the house back in the hands of a family member and the museum in a location that was better for it than the house could ever be.

Yes, Gina decided, a quarter of a million dollars would be more than fair to Dez. Not that she planned to make a counteroffer right away. She'd let him sweat just a little. Let him wonder if the house might slide through his grasp after all. And even when she did make a move, she would offer him only part of the money, just to see what he said.

In any case, before she could start throwing those kinds of figures around, she'd need to have a pretty good idea of where the money was coming from.

It didn't take a genius to see that holding a village fair in Essie's garden wasn't going to raise that kind of cash. And to add to the problem, getting hold of the option would be only the first step on the road. She would still have to talk Tyler-Royale into donating the store, and then there would be costs to adapt the building and move the museum...

She had some serious fund-raising to do. To get the kind of money she needed, she was going to have to take her case to the public. Carla could help with that, and Anne Garrett...

Though it was too bad Dez hadn't gone for the hot tub idea. That would have been the easiest ten thousand dollars she'd ever raise.

Visitor traffic in the museum had picked up because of Anne Garrett's article in the *Chronicle* and Carla's television coverage of the whole Tyler-Royale controversy, and some days it seemed to Gina that Essie's house was bulging at the seams.

It had always been difficult to find enough volunteers to guide all the tours, and now it was impossible. But it was equally unthinkable to turn away visitors who had cash in hand—especially when they'd need every dollar they could raise.

Gina was spending most of the museum's open hours walking from room to room and trying to keep an eye on everybody. It was an impractical plan, but it was the best she could do.

Inevitably, there were problems. The bored child of inattentive parents knocked over a Civil-War-era camera in the photography display upstairs, shattering the glass in the brass-barreled lens. When Gina asked the parents to be more careful, the father told her that it was her own fault for having a too-crowded exhibit.

Gina bit her tongue hard, and when she could control her voice again, she said, "We're trying to do something about that right now. If you'd care to make a donation toward a more spacious museum, I'd be happy to accept your check."

The couple looked at her as if she'd sprouted horns, and moved off to the next exhibit.

Gina sighed.

Eleanor had come running at the sound of the crash, still holding a dust cloth. "Makes you wonder sometimes if it's worth all the effort," she muttered. "Go and sit down, Gina. I can dust and ride herd on this bunch at the same time—don't forget I've got a couple of kids of my own."

"Yours aren't like this one," Gina muttered. But she gratefully accepted the help and headed for the kitchen to get a cold drink.

She didn't get that far. In the entrance hall, a beleaguered volunteer was surrounded by what looked like a seething mass of piranhas in a pool. Startled, Gina looked again and realized it was only a group of children, about kindergarten age—a class they hadn't been expecting. Each of the children was jumping up and down, holding up a hand full of cash, and demanding to be first. Their chaperon was earnestly explaining to the volunteer that it was a learning experience for each one of them to buy their own individual tickets.

Just beyond them, lounging against the door with his arms folded across his chest and looking both patient and dangerous, was Dez Kerrigan.

Gina tried to avoid making eye contact with him. *First things first,* she thought.

"Get in a line," she called, and the noise level dropped a little. "I'll take care of the money, Beth," she told the volunteer, "and you stamp their hands as each one pays. Then I'll take over here for a while, so you can show them through the exhibits."

The volunteer looked as if she'd rather submit to having lighted matches stuck under her toenails.

Gina didn't blame her. But if Dez had come to talk about

the trade, she could hardly put him on hold. She'd deal with him first. Then as soon as she could she'd catch up and take over as tour guide—and maybe Beth wouldn't quit altogether.

"What fun," Beth said under her breath, and as soon as the last little hand surrendered the last grubby wad of bills, she shepherded the group up the stairs.

The staircase creaked as the group bounced on every step.

"Sounds pretty threatening," Dez said. "And it's only a bunch of little kids."

"They're small, but they're energetic. And there are a lot of them."

"You should have Nate take a good look at the supports under there."

"I'll keep it in mind. But of course the stairs weren't built to handle crowds."

"That's exactly my point."

Gina went smoothly on. "Not like the Tyler-Royale building was, at any rate. That's why it would be so perfect for a museum... What can I do for you today?"

"I came to buy a ticket for the village fair."

Is that all? "If you're going to ask me to break a big bill, I hope you don't mind getting lots of small change."

"I'll write a check."

"Good choice—much more sanitary than taking home dollar bills smeared with heaven knows what. Pizza sauce, for one." Gina opened a cabinet under the stairs and pulled out the metal ticket box devoted to the village fair. "Have you thought any more about my offer?"

"Which one?" Dez didn't look up from his checkbook.

Gina pretended she hadn't heard him. The whole hot tub issue would be far better forgotten—only a momentary madness had made her mention it in the first place. She brushed dust off the top of the box. "I'm afraid that half a million is more than the board will agree to spend—considering that they wouldn't have much to show for it."

"Then they won't get the option." Dez tore out the check and handed it over.

"But I'm sure if you'd consider lowering the price—"

"To what?" he asked pleasantly.

Gina bit back a smile. He was interested; he couldn't hide it. "I think they'd go for a hundred and fifty thousand. And Essie's house, of course."

"Oh, I hadn't forgotten that part. A hundred and fifty, hmm?"

The silence stretched out and was broken by the thunder of small feet in the room over their heads. She held up his ticket.

"From nothing to a hundred and fifty in just a few days," Dez said finally. "That's not bad. A couple more jumps like that and you'll be in my neighborhood." He took the ticket from her hand.

Gina was stunned. "You're not even willing to negotiate?"

"I told you my price, sweetheart."

"But the real estate market doesn't work that way. It never has. The first time a Neanderthal asked his neighbor how many animal skins he wanted in order to trade caves, the neighbor asked for twice as many as he thought he'd actually get!"

"I'd point out that I'm not a Neanderthal, but I suspect that would only start an argument. I should correct myself—I actually didn't tell you my price. I said that was the lowest figure I'd even consider. So unless you're going to talk half a million dollars—"

"You'd rather I not waste your time," Gina finished.

"You want to negotiate in reverse, don't you? If I'd offer you what you asked, you'd raise it."

"Probably. Give it up, Gina. You aren't going to get that building."

"Maybe not," she said. "But one thing is sure. I can make it positively mortifying for you if you try to destroy it."

He flicked the ticket across her cheek. The serrated edge, where she'd torn it from the booklet, tickled her skin.

"Give it a whirl and see what happens," he said. "At least it'll keep you busy."

Gina was at the television station early, waiting in a small room just outside the studio where the local-interest current affairs program was aired. She was trying to keep her mind occupied with a magazine, when Carla swooped in and dropped into the next chair.

Gina felt a surge of relief. "I didn't know you were going to be hosting the talk show tonight."

"I'm not. I'm only here because I have to put together a piece about the dog show for the late news." Carla rolled her eyes. "A dog show, of all things. It's been a slow news day—you'll get good coverage on your fund-raising pitch. I see you took my advice about how to dress."

Gina smoothed a hand over her dark blue suit. "I wish you were hosting."

"It's Jason's show and he's terrific at it. Just relax, you'll be fine. Did you bring some exhibit stuff? Show-and-tell is always good."

Gina pointed to a box on the table next to her. "I'd hoped to talk to the host beforehand about the things I brought and the points I want to make."

Carla shook her head. "Jason never talks to a guest before the show starts—the conversation is always fresher and better that way. It's more interesting, and more lively.''

"And more surprising,'' Gina said glumly. "Particularly for the guest.''

Carla smiled. "Just relax and answer his questions. Tell him about the things you've brought—you really sparkle when you're talking about history. Oh, here you go.''

A young woman was leaning into the room. ''Ms. Haskell? Jason's ready for you now.''

But am I ready for him? Gina squared her shoulders and tried not to think about how important it was that she make a good impression on the viewers tonight. They were the ones who would decide—through their contributions—what the future of the museum would be.

She forgot her box and had to go back for it. So when she finally settled into her chair on the set, with the box on a low table beside her, there was only a minute to go till the show went on the air, and the crew spent most of that time fiddling with the microphone they'd put on her earlier. Despite what the assistant had said, the host was nowhere to be seen.

Gina still hadn't quite got her breath when the door opened again. The host came in with a flourish, flicked his microphone into place with one hand, and glanced down at the bare desk in front of him. "Where are my notes?'' he called. "Who do we have on the show tonight?''

Gina tried not to wince. If he didn't even know who she was, much less why she was there... *This is going to be a disaster.*

A young female assistant handed Jason a sheet of paper and ducked off the set just as the camera's red light glared straight into Gina's eyes.

Jason said smoothly, "Good evening, and welcome to *Current Affairs*. Our guest tonight is Gina Haskell of the

Kerrigan County Historical Museum, here to talk about her quest to save the Tyler-Royale building from its threatened destruction. Ms. Haskell, tell us how your interest in the department store began.''

But that's not why I'm here, Gina wanted to say. Then she thought better of it. Carla had said the man knew what he was doing; perhaps it would be better if she played along. Maybe he was just using Tyler-Royale as a springboard to build audience interest before he got into the museum's need to raise money.

"I've always been interested in the building," she said. "I think everybody in Lakemont has walked through that store and marveled at the atrium, with its stained-glass dome and mosaic floor."

The anchor nodded. "With that enormous red rose inlaid right smack in the middle. 'Meet me on the rose,'" he quoted. "It makes you wonder where people will choose as a meeting place if the building is destroyed. 'Meet me by the mailbox on the corner' doesn't have nearly the same charm."

Gina smiled. "It almost sounds like a book title, doesn't it? *Meet Me On the Rose—Memories of Tyler-Royale.*" She hoped Dez was watching this. The very idea of a book celebrating the landmark he was personally aiming to destroy should kick his heartburn into high gear.

"That's a good one. Tell me, Gina—may I call you Gina?—what's your strongest memory of the rose? Meeting your mother there on a shopping trip, perhaps?"

The question took her off guard, and she spoke too quickly; her voice was almost a squeak. "No." She took a breath and forced herself to smile. "No—my strongest memory is of meeting a date there, when I was in college."

Jason's gaze was bright and inquisitive, and Gina felt a

flicker of fear. But he didn't push the question. "How is it going—the campaign to save the building?"

Miserably. "I've met with Mr. Kerrigan a number of times, and we're discussing the possibilities."

"I understand one potential use for the building is to house the Kerrigan County Historical Museum. Your museum."

"Well, I wouldn't call it mine, personally. It belongs to all the people of Kerrigan County. But yes, that's one of the possibilities that Mr. Kerrigan and I have touched on." *Here's my chance,* Gina thought. "You see, the museum really needs more space. Whether we move into a different building or put an addition on the one we currently have is yet to be decided, but we're asking for donations from the public to allow us to acquire more room—one way or the other."

"Well, that's a worthwhile cause—particularly if it helps save the Tyler-Royale building. Put me down for a pledge—we'll talk about the amount later."

"With pleasure," Gina said.

"You've been involved with the museum for a number of years, I understand. Tell us how you got so interested in history."

Gina relaxed a little. At last they were onto familiar ground. "My history teacher in middle school was Essie Kerrigan, who single-handedly started the historical society and the museum."

Jason's eyebrows rose a little. "Well, my middle school history teacher was a bit of a crank, too, but that didn't make me an historian."

"Well, perhaps I was predisposed to like the subject. But I enjoyed hearing about the things she owned—take her cookie jar, for instance." Gina reached into the box and carefully lifted the pottery jar out of its protective paper wrapping. Under the strong studio lights, the blue glaze looked almost purple. "Essie bought it at an antiques shop here in town for just a few dollars, simply because she liked the shape of it. But it had an unusual mark on the bottom." She tipped it up, and the camera obligingly zoomed in. "She kept looking for the explanation of that mark, and when she discovered that it was the potter's initials, she realized what an unusual piece it was. It's quite rare, in fact—it's one of the first pieces of pottery ever made in Kerrigan County."

"And she was using it as a cookie jar? Of course, as soon as she realized it was valuable, she must have put a stop to that."

"Oh, no. It had cookies in it till the day she died." Gina laughed at the expression on Jason's face. "That was what was so unusual about Essie. She lived with her collection, she used her possessions—and she passed along not only love of her things but of their history. That was truly a gift for someone who had very little history of her own—"

Someone like me.

She stopped abruptly, realizing that Jason's eyes had brightened once more and his nose was practically twitching at the scent of an interesting story. Now she was in for it. If he started to probe... She'd better try to gloss it over before he began asking questions.

She took a deep breath. "I was raised in foster homes, so I really didn't have any family stories. Essie shared hers with me." She set the pottery jar back in the box.

"You mean stories like how great-granddad came over on the boat, and Uncle Harry went to Alaska in the Gold Rush and never came back?"

"Every family has its private fairy tales."

"So because you didn't know your own, you borrowed the Kerrigan family legends."

"I suppose you could put it that way. I certainly know them all by heart." She dug into the box again. "I've also brought a few things from the prehistoric period—a stone ax and some arrowheads that were found in western Kerrigan County. We have a lot of prehistoric items in the collection, but we don't have gallery space to show them right now. In a new building, or a new wing, we could have these visible all the time."

Jason's gaze held a tinge of sympathy, Gina thought, as well as a good deal of admiration for the way she'd changed the subject. It might not have been terribly smooth, but it had been effective.

"I must say I'm not a big fan of stone axes," he admitted. "What else do you have in that box?"

Gina pulled out an ivory-colored card, the shape of a fan, with a faded pink ribbon dangling. "This is a dance card from the first Carousel Ball, over a hundred years ago," she said. "Every debutante at the ball had a card, and young men signed their names in the spaces to claim their dances. The ribbon let the debutante wear it dangling from her wrist while she danced. This one belonged to Essie Kerrigan's mother, and that ball was where she first met her future husband."

"Quite a lot different than how couples court these days," Jason mused.

Gina smiled. "Yes, it is. She probably had two chaperones keeping an eye on her that night. I was surprised to learn that the dance that year was held in the brand-new Tyler-Royale building. We found a group photograph of the debutantes, and it's clearly taken in the atrium—they're standing on the rose."

"Really?" Jason stretched out a hand for the photograph. "I wonder why they let that tradition die."

"Probably because the dance was held before the store

opened, so the building was still pretty much empty. It would be much more difficult to make it work these days— though I understand there's some interest in holding this year's ball there as well, if Mr. Kerrigan will allow it.''

"Tell you what," Jason said. "Let's ask him."

"Of course, just as the Carousel Ball was the very first use of the building," Gina said, "it could end up being the very last use as well, if— *What* did you say?''

Jason was gesturing to the young woman who'd handed him his notes at the start of the show. She ducked around the camera crew and went to the studio door.

"We've invited Dez Kerrigan to join the discussion tonight," Jason said smoothly, "since he's the only one who knows the answers concerning the Tyler-Royale building."

If he'd picked up the stone ax and whacked her with it, Gina couldn't have been more shocked. *I've been ambushed,* she thought.

Why hadn't Carla warned her? Unless Carla hadn't known, either. From what she'd said, Jason seemed to like surprises....

Dez crossed the set with an unhurried stride and shook Jason's hand. Gina, determined to be a good sport, offered her hand too, but instead of shaking it, Dez raised it to his mouth.

She couldn't help it; her fingers clenched into a fist. He brushed each tight knuckle with his lips, and smiled at her as he released her hand. "Hello, Gina.''

"Nice to see you, Dez.''

"That's good," said Jason, sounding gleeful. "The formalities have been observed and now you can both come out of your corners swinging. Dez, what about the Carousel Ball? Will it be held in the Tyler-Royale atrium as Gina suggests?''

"You'd have to talk to the committee in charge of the

dance, I'm afraid. Or perhaps someone at Tyler-Royale. Until the store actually closes, I don't have anything to say about what happens there."

"But that won't be long now, will it?" Jason asked. "The final sales are well under way."

"No one's given me a date."

"And when you take possession, how soon will you be doing something with the site?"

"I'm not sure I'll be doing anything," Dez said. "Don't forget that I don't actually own it yet."

"As if you'd give up that option money," Gina muttered, "and get nothing back for it."

Dez casually rested a fingertip on the microphone clipped to his tie. "At least then I'd know exactly what it would cost me. On the other hand, if I trade it for Essie's house, I'm only getting started."

"Dez," Jason said, "I'm afraid you're blocking your microphone. What were you saying?"

"But think of what you'd have," Gina said.

"Believe me, I've thought." He smiled at Jason. "So sorry. Careless of me. What was the question again?"

"There's talk around town that you're considering building an apartment tower."

"There's always talk around town. It would be premature to make announcements of any kind."

Jason bored in. "But you intend to demolish the building."

"I said, no announcements of *any* kind."

"Just think about what a monument it would be to your cgo if you preserved it," Gina said. This time she didn't bother to keep her voice low.

"And yours, if you could boast that you'd single-handedly saved it."

Jason was grinning.

"My main interest is the museum and what's best for it," Gina said firmly. "It always has been."

Jason rubbed his hands together in glee. "Yes, what about the museum, Dez? You must have some personal interest in it. Was it your grandmother who started it?"

"Great-aunt," Dez said. "Essie was my grandfather's sister."

"You actually know that much about the family tree?" Gina said under her breath.

He gave her what must, Gina thought, be his most charming smile. "Yes, but you'll have to fill me in on the legends sometime." Turning back to Jason, he said, "Of course I want to see the museum continue and be successful. However, it's land-locked where it is, so the most sensible course is to move it out of the current building."

"Into the Tyler-Royale store?" Jason asked eagerly.

"I'm not going to take a stand on where it should go. That's up to the museum board to decide. But I'll happily make a pledge to the fund-raising campaign."

Gina blinked. "You will? That's very—"

"A few days ago you made me a proposition concerning a hot tub," Dez said.

Me and my big mouth.

"If you'll get into it with me, Gina, I'll pledge a hundred dollars—"

She grasped at the figure with relief. "Only a hundred?" she jeered. "That's hardly worth the effort."

"A hundred dollars for every minute you stay in."

Jason said, "Well, Gina? What about it? Sounds to me like a pretty easy way to make money."

She had to give him credit; Dez had boxed her in so neatly that there was only one thing to do. She gritted her teeth for a moment, and then forced herself to smile. "Fine. Name the time and the place and I'll be there."

"Friday night, eight o'clock," Dez said. "Under the stained-glass dome."

Stained glass… Gina gasped. "At *Tyler-Royale?*"

"Yes, darling," Dez said, his voice silky. "Meet me on the rose."

CHAPTER EIGHT

JASON looked as if he was going to need a forklift to get his jaw back in place. Gina understood only too well how he felt.

"At the st-store?" she stammered.

Dez's eyebrows rose. "Since Tyler-Royale is donating the use of the hot tub, it didn't seem reasonable for me to ask them to move it across town as well."

Since when have you worried about being reasonable? "I thought—"

"That we were going to use my own personal private tub," he agreed. "I thought so too, and I know how much you were looking forward to it."

Gina thought she was going to choke.

"But then I realized that a private little splash—just the two of us—wouldn't do the museum much good. And once I started thinking of the promotional possibilities and how we could use this for the good of the museum, everything just mushroomed."

He sounds positively sanctimonious, Gina thought. *Talking about the good of the museum—as if he cares!*

"As soon as I suggested it to the Tyler-Royale people, they fell in love with the idea. The manager figures it will draw the biggest crowd downtown Lakemont has seen in years." Dez paused for a moment, and then added gently, "The CEO's even matching my pledge."

That raised the stakes to two hundred dollars per minute. Gina swallowed hard.

He had already very carefully pointed out to every last

viewer that the hot tub had been her idea in the first place—
so if she turned the offer down now, she might as well call
off the fund-raising campaign altogether, because nobody
would ever again take her seriously. She had to admire the
neat construction of the trap he'd sprung, even while she
frantically looked for any possible way out.

But she knew better than to think she'd find one. He'd
had days to create this snare, and he'd deliberately left her
only minutes to react to it.

"It's a deal," she said. Her voice seemed to be coming
from a great distance. "Eight o'clock Friday, in the
atrium."

Jason seemed, at long last, to have regained control of
his jaw. "You'll certainly have a new, long-lasting memory
of meeting on the rose, Gina. You told us earlier that Essie
Kerrigan's mom probably had two chaperones keeping an
eye on her the night she danced there. You'll no doubt have
two hundred watching you take a bath there."

Oh, that really makes me feel better.

"Instead of a dance card," Dez said dreamily, "you can
have them all sign your pledge card. Better make it a big
one."

Jason turned to face the camera. "Well, folks, there you
have it—the show tonight has truly been a *Current Affair*.
And don't worry—if you can't make it downtown yourself
on Friday night, just tune to this station because we'll have
a camera crew on hand."

The red lights on the cameras blinked off. "Thanks for
a great show," Jason said. "You two—honestly. What a
performance!" He breezed off the set.

Gina sagged in her chair and put her head in her hands.

"Would you like a drink of water?" Dez asked help-
fully. "A jolt of caffeine? A slug of vodka?"

"The only thing I want," she said between clenched teeth, "is never to see you again."

Dez didn't seem to hear her. He was looking at the contents of the box on the table beside her. "If it isn't my old friend the cookie jar," he murmured. "Am I allowed to touch it?"

Gina waved a hand in consent. If she picked up the jar right now, she realized, she'd be apt to crown him with it.

She'd simply set the jar into the box. He wrapped it once more in its protective paper, stowed it safely, and picked up the box.

"I'll take that," she said automatically.

"It's no problem. How did you get all this down here, anyway?"

"The same way I'll get it back to the museum—in a cab."

"I'll give you a ride."

"No, thank you."

"Donate the cab fare to the museum fund."

Since he'd put it that way, Gina could hardly be ungracious enough to refuse. Besides, she had a few things to tell him that would not be smart to say inside any building that housed cameras and recording equipment. "You can just drop me at home—I'll take the box back to the museum tomorrow."

He put the box into the back of his car and helped her in. Gina stared straight forward as the car pulled into traffic. "Whatever inspired you to bring Tyler-Royale into this, anyway?"

"It was a natural. Actually, I thought about The Maple Tree first."

"The restaurant? *Why?*"

"Because it was where we first met." The sentimental note in his voice was so sweet that it practically sent Gina into sugar overload. "But they can't fit in as big a crowd, and therefore the cover charge would have to be pretty steep. However, considering that this is really all about Tyler-Royale in the first place— Why are you taking this so personally, anyway? People get into hot tubs together all the time without necessarily being intimate friends."

That was true enough, Gina admitted. In hotels, perfect strangers shared spas and whirlpools without a second thought. Even at private pool parties, the people cavorting around in swimsuits weren't always pals. Why was she making such a production out of it?

There's nothing to it, really. All I have to do is get into a small tank of warm, bubbly water, stay there just as long as I can keep myself from killing him, and get out. And the museum fund will be hundreds—maybe thousands—of dollars richer.

It didn't help.

She was taking it so personally, Gina concluded, because from the very beginning Dez had implied that getting into a hot tub with him would be much more than a casual soak to soothe an aching spine. And when he talked about being intimate friends—well, his emphasis was hardly on the friendship part.

Of course, she mused, *with two hundred chaperones observing every move, it's hardly going to be intimate.*

"Unless you want it to be personal," he said. "Now there's an interesting thought."

She pretended to ignore him. "I guess it's just because I'm not used to parading around in public in a swimsuit. If I'd only realized what was in my future, I'd have entered the Miss America pageant just for practice. But I still want to know what prompted you to turn this event into a circus."

He shrugged. "You said it would take ten thousand dollars to get you into a hot tub. You didn't specify that it had to be *my* ten grand. So I got to thinking that if you aren't going to allow any of the really interesting ways to pass time in a hot tub—''

"You're absolutely right—unless reading a book is on your list.''

"Too soggy. Anyway, if you aren't going to allow yourself to have fun, then you might as well maximize the financial impact of the stunt. Never settle for ten grand when you might collect twenty-five.''

"That much? Do you really think so?'' *How many minutes would that be?*

He shot a look at her. "Greedy little thing, aren't you? Your eyes are positively glowing at the idea. I wasn't joking about the pledge card, either. I'm sure we can pick up a little extra action on the side. In fact, as long as we're talking about you parading around in a swimsuit—''

"Don't even *think* about suggesting I strut around the store wearing one.''

"You could put a sandwich board over it that says, 'Come Watch The Kerrigan County Historical Museum Make A Splash.'''

"That's too long to be a good slogan.''

"True. And having you walking around in a swimsuit wasn't what I was going to suggest anyway.''

"If it's worse than that, I *really* don't want to hear what you were thinking about.''

He didn't pause. "I was thinking that this whole thing would be more fun without swimsuits.''

"In your dreams, Kerrigan.'' *Unless...* It had been pretty careless of him not to specify restrictions on what she could wear instead of a suit. Unusually careless, in fact.

He seemed to read her mind. "Hold it right there, Gina. I didn't mean you could get into the water in your street clothes. You get in the tub and then hand me your swimsuit, and I'll pay two hundred dollars a minute.''

"You don't think I'll do it, do you?"

"I guess we'll see." He didn't sound as if the question concerned him much. "Just leave the box in the car— I'll drop it off at the museum on my way to work in the morning.''

"If you're sure you don't mind. You don't have to walk me to the door, Dez.''

"Wouldn't miss it for the world." He parked by the curb in front of her row house and got out of the car.

On the front porch he said, "Ready for lesson two?"

No. In fact, I'm planning to drop that class.

But then he would imagine that she felt threatened by a good-night kiss. It would only inflate his ego further, and the last thing the man needed was encouragement in that department.

"Why?" she asked instead. "Are you having trouble finding study partners?"

He smiled and draped an arm around her shoulders. Then he leaned back against the porch pillar. As if, Gina thought, he didn't want to have to think about keeping his balance— so he could devote all his attention to her.

There was an odd sort of flutter in the pit of her stomach, now that it was too late to back out. Slowly he drew her closer, until she was standing only a breath away. In the cool evening air, the warmth of his body acted like a magnet.

His lips were cool, grazing the line of her jaw, her earlobe, her cheekbone. Her eyelids fluttered, and closed. She intended to stay perfectly still, but instead she found herself turning her head to meet his kiss.

She could feel his lips curve in amusement. Aggravated by her own half-conscious complicity, she tried to pull out of his arms. But her will seemed to have drained away under that gentle touch, and she could no longer move.

He kissed her long and softly, and then the tip of his tongue teased against her lips, and she relaxed and let him deepen the kiss.

He kissed her forever, and yet it was not long enough. When he stopped, she would have protested—except that she'd completely lost the power of speech.

Dez ran a fingertip down the side of her face and said, "You've been doing your homework." His voice sounded just a little unsteady.

The front door opened. Gina tried to focus her eyes, but for a moment she wasn't sure what she was seeing. Her downstairs neighbor, that much was clear—but what was Mrs. Mason doing?

The woman was wearing a loud tartan-plaid dressing gown, and her hair was in curlers. In her hand was a wire carrier holding four squat glass bottles. "Excuse me," she said tartly. "But you're standing right where the milk bottles go."

Gina tried to move out of the way and lost her balance. Dez put his hands on her shoulders to hold her perpendicular.

As if he thinks I can't stand up on my own, Gina thought. The fact that he was right was beside the point.

Mrs. Mason set her empty bottles next to the porch pillar, looked Dez and Gina up and down, sniffed, and went back in, shutting the door with a firm thump.

Gina frowned. "She's demented. Do you have any idea how many years it's been since there was regular milk delivery in this neighborhood?"

Dez was laughing. "No, but I'll bet Mrs. Mason knows. You don't seriously think that had anything to do with milk bottles, do you? Come here."

Gina shook her head and bent over the wire carrier to inspect the bottles. "I'll have to ask her to donate them to the museum. We don't have any from this particular dairy."

Dez sighed. "That trims me down to size—coming in second to a quartet of milk bottles. See you tomorrow."

He was whistling softly as he walked down the sidewalk.

Thank you, Mrs. Mason, Gina thought. That lesson of his had been so devastatingly effective that she'd been on the point of inviting Dez upstairs for the final exam.

As if the fact that the man kissed like an angel meant that making love with him wouldn't be a devilishly bad idea.

Get in the tub and hand me your swimsuit, and I'll pay two hundred dollars a minute.

She might as well take him up on it. Because in truth it wouldn't matter what she wore into the tub.

Bathing suit. Street clothes. Suit of armor... No matter what she put on, Dez could make it feel like nothing at all.

Gina had forgotten Carla's careless comment, before the television show began, about it having been a very slow news day, with few important stories to cover. But the reporter had been right. Every media outlet in Lakemont jumped on the hot tub story and ran with it.

Anne Garrett, stopping by the museum at midafternoon on Thursday, found Gina at the admissions stand in the main hallway and looked her over admiringly. "No wonder you haven't set up a lunch date so we can plan your fundraising campaign. This caper makes everything I've considered look pretty tame."

"I'm sorry about the lunch," Gina said hastily. "It's been awfully busy around here. But we're still going to need all your ideas, because I can't stay in that tub long enough to collect all the money we'll need.''

''Why on earth not?'' Anne murmured. ''From all appearances, you look forward to getting yourself in hot water. And you do it so well, too. Oh, all right, I'll keep thinking. But this is going to be a very tough act to follow.''

''Actually, before you go off and start brainstorming… I don't know all that much about hot tubs. Can you help me figure out how much bubble bath to put in? I need enough bubbles to cover the whole surface, but I don't want suds overflowing all over the atrium. Or suffocating me, either, if it comes to that.''

Anne shook her head. ''You can't put bubble bath in a whirlpool tub—I think it's because it'll clog up the jets. What's wrong with just plain warm water, anyway?''

''It's transparent.''

''Sort of like your face, you mean. You're turning very pink all of a sudden. No bubbles—the store people would have a collective stroke. But there's something else that might do the trick—''

Gina heard the door creak open and caught a glimpse of blue-black hair. She held up both hands, silently pleading for Anne to say no more.

Dez came in with Gina's box of museum treasures held casually under one arm. ''It makes me suspicious whenever I see you two with your heads together but not talking. Sorry I didn't get your box delivered this morning, Gina. I had a crisis.''

''That's all right. Only one person asked about the cookie jar today, and he said he'd come back some other time.''

''I'm relieved. Don't let me interrupt, by the way.''

''Oh, I need to run along,'' Anne said cheerfully. ''I just

came by to pick up some tickets for the village fair. There's no sense in talking to people about the event if I can't guilt-trip them into buying a ticket right then.''

Gina got the ticket box out from under the stairs and wiped off the top with a tissue. ''One pack?''

''Why bother with only one? Give me ten at least. Want me to sign for them?'' Anne reached for Gina's pen. ''Give me that receipt book.'' She signed with a flourish, flipped the booklet shut, and handed it back to Gina. ''You can finish filling it out later.'' She flashed a smile at Dez and was gone.

Without suggesting what I can use instead of bubble bath, Gina thought glumly. She started to put the tickets away. ''Want to take some tickets, Dez? If you don't think you can sell them, they'd make great employee incentives.''

''Thanks, but I believe I'm already doing my part to support the museum. Have you bought your new swimsuit yet?''

''How did you—'' She stopped.

Dez was grinning. ''Because no woman worth thinking about would get into that tub in an old one, that's why. And sweetheart, you are definitely worth thinking about.'' He moved the box he'd carried inside to a safer spot on the ledge between the pillars which separated the entrance hall from the enormous living room. Then he put his index finger under Gina's chin, turned her face up, and kissed her.

''Was that lesson three?'' Gina asked calmly.

''No, dear. Neither one of us has time for lesson three just now. That was only a pop quiz to keep you fresh.''

He'd been gone for several minutes when Gina started to put away the ticket box and remembered the receipt Anne had signed. She'd better write down the numbers of the ticket books Anne had taken, because in the press of things she was likely to forget.

But Anne hadn't signed her name on the receipt. Instead, she'd written two simple words—the phrase she'd no doubt been about to utter when Dez had walked in and interrupted. The answer to Gina's question.

The perfect answer.

"Eleanor!" Gina called, and the volunteer leaned over the railing of the upstairs landing. "Can you handle things for a while? I need to go shopping."

The cabbie who picked up Gina in front of the museum on Friday evening was obviously curious about the contents of the three enormous black plastic garbage bags she was carrying, particularly when she had trouble fitting them through the back door of the cab. By the time her packages were finally stowed, there wasn't enough room left for Gina, so she got in the front seat.

"You know, I took a clown to a birthday party once," the cabbie mused. "Had all kinds of trouble getting his helium balloons in the car. Must have been a hundred of them. And once a buddy of mine took a guy with a bunch of garbage bags up to a boat ramp twenty miles north of town. It turned out later he was dumping a body in the lake. Well, pieces of it, anyway."

Gina winced.

"But I guess what you've got isn't heavy enough to be a body, or light enough to be balloons," he said.

"Congratulations," Gina said. "You guessed right."

He waited a while in hopeful silence before he finally said, "So what is it?"

"Oh, you'll have far more fun speculating than if you actually knew. I wouldn't want to ruin your fun. You can drop me at the front entrance—that will be fine."

There were already two television-station trucks parked outside Tyler-Royale, satellite dishes at the ready. But at least the entrance wasn't thronged with people. Maybe that meant all the predictions had been wrong and the public was entirely indifferent to the whole question of hot tubs.

The bad part of that, Gina thought, was that if this ploy wasn't enough to get their attention, they might not give much thought to the rest of the fund-raising campaign, either.

Don't be such a pessimist, she told herself. *Maybe they're just staying home to watch it on TV.*

She excavated her bags from the back of the cab, paid the cabbie, and said, "If you really can't stand the suspense of not knowing what's in the bags, check out the late news on Channel Five."

Comprehension dawned in his face. "Oh, you're part of *that*," he said. "I told my wife to record it all so I can watch when I get home."

"I hope you won't be disappointed," Gina murmured.

One of the television crew held the door for her, and another offered to put her bags atop the cart full of equipment he was getting ready to roll in. But Gina declined with a smile. Anybody who thought she'd let the precious contents of these bags out of her hands, much less out of her sight, had to be crazy. After the trouble she'd had getting hold of them...

She turned the corner between cosmetics and shoes, saw the atrium open up ahead of her, and stopped dead.

The entrance hadn't been practically deserted because of a lack of interest. It was because the crowd had already gathered, apparently anxious to make sure they had the best possible view. The atrium was almost standing-room-only, and all the way to the top of the building, every balcony was lined.

"A hot-dog vendor could do a booming business," Gina muttered.

It took a while to work her way through the crowd, considering that with her bags she took up the same amount of room as ten ordinary people. But finally she reached the center. On top of the mosaic rose, covering it entirely, was the tub, already set up and running.

A very big tub—so big that there was a short flight of steps next to it, to aid in getting in and out. A bright red, heart-shaped tub.

I should have expected he'd choose something like that, she thought. She only hoped three bags full would be enough.

Dez didn't see her come in; the press of the crowd prevented that. But he knew she was there, because some internal radar had gone crazy the moment she'd reached the atrium. Or perhaps, he reassured himself, it wasn't really Gina that he'd sensed but the changed attitude of the crowd as they recognized her. Yes, that would be it—the noise level had dropped and then risen excitedly. That was what he'd reacted to—not Gina herself.

Unhurriedly, he continued to work the crowd, trading teasing barbs, collecting pledges, and answering questions, and only when he'd circled the entire atrium did he come back to the side of the tub.

Gina was standing there waiting for him, wearing a terrycloth robe and looking extraordinarily pleased with herself. On the tile floor at her feet lay three empty black plastic garbage bags. And in the tub...

He had to look a second time to convince himself that he wasn't seeing things.

In the tub floated hundreds—maybe thousands—of plastic toys. Or maybe *floated* wasn't quite the right word, because there were so many of them that some were stacked on top of each other, not even touching the water.

At a glance he could see at least a hundred ducks. Not ordinary ducks, either. There were red ducks, blue ducks, purple ducks, green ducks, and a few ordinary yellow ducks. There were ducks sporting sunglasses, ducks with snorkels, ducks in nightcaps, ducks wearing tutus, ducks in sunbonnets, ducks riding rafts, ducks wearing headphones, and ducks balanced on water-skis. There was a duck that looked vaguely like Marilyn Monroe, and one right on top of the pile that was wearing a life-jacket stamped *Titanic*.

But she hadn't just filled the tub with ducks. Bobbing up and down alongside was every other sort of water-loving creature as well. Dolphins, whales, seahorses, sharks, pelicans, Canadian geese, fish of every shape and color, and a whole brood of penguins. He wouldn't be surprised, if he reached in, to find a plastic clamshell clamped to his finger.

And then there were the boats. Small plastic rowboats, tugboats, cabin cruisers, wind-up submarines...

How had Gina managed to buy up every floating toy in the city of Lakemont without him getting wind of it? And there was no doubt in his mind that was exactly what she'd done. It would take a shovel to move enough of the floating debris so a person could get in. And once in, a body could get lost under layers of toys...

Which, of course, was the entire point of the flotilla.

"That's my girl," he said. "You're actually going to do it."

"Of course. I'm just applying your own philosophy, Dez. It would be foolish to settle for a hundred dollars a minute when I can get two hundred. And that's just from you. I'm not even counting the other pledges." She shrugged off the robe and let it pool at her feet. Underneath it was a two-piece, neon-pink swimsuit. It was so bright that it almost glowed.

"However," she said primly, "I'm sure you'll remember that you said I could get in the tub first, and then hand you my suit."

"Damn," Dez said.

"No changing your mind now. You were very specific." From the top of the steps beside the tub, she stuck in one foot and wiggled a few toys out of the way. Then she climbed in and sank into the midst of the flotsam. Ducks piled up in heaps around her.

The crowd was almost silent, watching her. She seemed to be having trouble—not surprising, Dez thought. Taking a wet swimsuit off while staying underwater would be a challenge even without all the ducks getting in the way.

It took almost two minutes before a slender hand emerged from the water, holding up a dripping neon-pink swimsuit top. The crowd roared its approval.

Dez leaned over the edge of the tub and snagged the top by a shoulder strap. Despite the evidence of his own eyes, he still couldn't quite believe she'd done it. "That's good enough," he said. "You've proved yourself."

She gave him a wide-eyed look. "You're not going to back down on your offer to double your pledge, are you? Because if you're going to try to get by with a hundred and fifty a minute, I'll hand you the other half."

Dez surrendered. "You've got witnesses, Gina. Two hundred bucks a minute, starting now." He consulted the waterproof watch on his wrist. "It's twelve minutes past eight, and counting."

She gave him a gamine smile. "Come on in, the water's great."

If she hadn't teased him, he thought, he might have let it rest there. But that smile and the come-hither look in her eyes stirred up a pool of mischief inside him that had already been threatening to flood over.

He held up the swimsuit top. ''Now that Gina doesn't need this any more, let's have a little auction. All for the good of the museum, of course. What am I bid for one slightly used, very wet—''

He ignored the strangled protest from the tub. What was she going to do about it, anyway? Climb out and try to stop him?

He sold the swimsuit top to one of the television guys for three hundred dollars. With a deep sense of satisfaction, he slid out of his own robe—to a chorus of groans from the female half of the audience when they saw he was wearing trunks—and climbed into the tub.

He splashed a bit before he got comfortable. ''Except for trying not to inhale a duck,'' he said, ''this is very nice. You really are a sport, Gina. Maybe we can talk the store into donating the tub to the museum, now that it's a historic artifact.'' He held out both arms to form a dam to hold back the ducks, and tried to sail a tugboat across the few inches of open water by blowing on it. But the rest of the floating toys surged back, and he gave it up, settled back in the warm water, and closed his eyes.

If he only had a hazelnut coffee…and if he'd been smart enough to choose a smaller tub…life would be perfect.

It was thirty-nine minutes by Dez's stopwatch before Gina said, ''That's it. I've had enough. I'm practically boiled.''

A good bit of the crowd had drifted away, but there were still enough die-hards to make things interesting.

Dez opened his eyes. She did look a little pink. He wondered if it was heat, or contemplation of what came next. ''And just how are you going to get out?'' he asked lazily.

"You can't reach your robe. But if you ask me very nicely, I might climb out first and hand it to you."

Gina smiled at him, and in a sort of reverse dive, with her arms extended and her fingers pointed up, emerged from the water.

Dez blinked and looked again. She was wearing the neon-pink suit. All of it.

"Now wait a minute," he sputtered.

"You said, 'Get in the tub and hand me your suit,'" she quoted. "You didn't say it had to be the suit I was wearing at that moment—just that I own it. And I've even got the receipt to prove it's mine."

"You know perfectly well that was not what I meant."

"Really?" She looked so innocent that he wanted to drown her right there, before she could corrupt anyone else. "It was actually you who gave me the idea, Dez—asking me if I'd bought a new suit yet. So, while I was shopping, I just bought two."

"And sneaked one into the tub when you dumped all the floaty toys. No wonder it took you some time and fancy gyrations before you handed over that top—you had to find it at the bottom of the tub."

"It was a little more difficult than I'd planned on," she admitted. "The tub's bigger than I expected, you see. The other half of the suit's still down there somewhere, if you want to go diving."

But Dez wasn't listening. There was something just a little odd about her, as she stood there. Her skin looked blue, everywhere but her face—as if she'd just climbed out of very cold water.

But that wasn't possible. She should be pink all over—not only from the heat, but from pure shame at the stunt she'd pulled. Unless...

He reached for a blue duck. It slid out of his hand, leaving a white streak on the duck and blue coloring coating his palm.

"These weren't all intended to be bathtub toys," he said.

"No, there seemed to be a shortage of them around town. So I bought a few decorations from florists, and some from craft shops. Why?"

He held up his hand. "Because they obviously weren't intended to soak in warm water. Let's just hope it washes off of us like it does the ducks—or we're going to have a serious case of the blues."

CHAPTER NINE

ALMOST everyone on the museum's volunteer roster stopped in during the morning after the great hot tub event—even ones Gina hadn't seen in weeks. They gave various excuses, but she was convinced there was only one reason—every last one of them wanted to find out whether she'd managed to get rid of the blue dye yet.

In fact, it had taken her over an hour, and in desperation she'd finally ended up using a facial scrub from head to foot before she'd gotten back her normal color. How a dye which practically slid off a plastic duck could attach itself so firmly to skin was beyond her.

She took advantage of the opportunity to press onto each volunteer a book of tickets to the village fair, now only a few days away. She was handing out the last ones when Dez came in.

"You're looking fine," Gina told him.

"I thought for a while I was going to have to send myself to the dry cleaner's. I brought a check to pay my pledge to the museum fund."

Gina didn't move. "If you'd like, we could hold a ceremony at the fair in appreciation of your contribution. Even if I did earn every cent of the money."

"No, thanks, I'd rather duck that one."

"Cute."

"But I'm sure everybody else who pledged would be honored by the attention. *And* you could require that they all buy tickets in order to come and be recognized."

Gina stretched out a hand. "Two hundred dollars a minute, right?"

He held up the slip of paper, just out of her reach. "Against my better judgment, yes. I didn't even deduct anything for the swimsuit caper."

"You'd better not. In fact, I'd say you owe me extra for that. The leftover half a suit I still have is pretty useless."

"That's entirely the wrong attitude, Gina. Look at it as spare parts."

"I'll keep that in mind. I'd love to chat, but between one thing and another I have a lot to do today."

He gestured toward the box which she'd left sitting on the ledge between entrance hall and living room. "I see you haven't even put Essie's cookie jar back on display."

"I haven't had time since you brought it back." She started to pull papers out of the box. "So unless you want to talk about terms for our trade—"

"As a matter of fact—"

Gina pulled out the last of the paper wrappings, but there was no pottery cookie jar. Everything else she'd taken to the television studio was still in the box, but the jar was gone. "That's odd. I wonder if someone saw it sitting here and put it back upstairs."

But the jar was not in its accustomed spot. Eleanor, who had been the only volunteer in the museum all day Friday, said she hadn't touched it. "And you've been in the hallway since opening time this morning, Gina," she pointed out, "so none of the other volunteers could have moved it."

With half a dozen people looking, it didn't take long to search the museum—and to reach the inevitable conclusion. Essie's cookie jar had disappeared. When and how it had vanished, Gina couldn't begin to guess. It didn't matter much, anyway, because however it had happened, she was responsible.

Guilt surged through her veins, and unshed tears burned her eyelids. "It's my fault."

Dez, who had helped search and then settled quietly onto the ledge where the box had once rested, said, "I'm just as much to blame—I'm the one who brought it back at an inconvenient time instead of when I told you I would."

"No, I'm responsible. I left the box sitting there." *And I went shopping,* she reminded herself. She'd been so inspired by the two words Anne Garrett had written on that receipt—rubber ducks—that she'd forgotten everything else in her quest to collect every floating object in the city of Lakemont.

And so Essie's prized piece of pottery was gone.

"I should have put it back in the display immediately," Gina said.

"It wouldn't have been much safer upstairs," Dez pointed out. "In fact, it might have been even easier to steal. All someone would have to do is wait until they were alone in the room. They'd have only needed a minute."

"If you're trying to make me feel worse, Dez, it's working. I know the security around here stinks. It's one of the reasons we need to remodel or move."

"That's true enough. If somebody was determined to get the jar out of here, they'd have gotten it no matter where it was. Why they'd want it is beyond me, but—"

"Well, that's my fault too, isn't it?" Gina asked bitterly. "I'm the one who held it up on television to talk about how valuable it was." She leaned against the newel post, shoulders slumped. The volunteers, she noticed, all seemed to have melted away as if they didn't want to be involved.

Dez slid off the ledge. "Come on," he said. "Let's go up to your office."

''Why not?'' Gina muttered. ''There's nothing left worth stealing down here.''

''Knock it off, Gina. You've lost track of one of Essie's possessions, which means you have about fourteen thousand and seventy-six of them left.''

''But that was an important one,'' Gina said drearily.

''Important to her, or important to you?''

''Both.'' The flight of stairs had never seemed so long. She stopped halfway up and looked back at Dez, suspicion suddenly percolating through her veins. Was she absolutely certain the cookie jar had been in the box at all?

It had definitely been there when she'd left the television studio; she'd watched Dez wrap it safely and put it in the box. That meant it had gotten as far as his car. But when he'd brought the box into the museum a day later, had she looked inside? Had she even touched the box? She remembered him carrying it in under his arm, as if it were only feather-weight, and setting it on the ledge...

This is nuts, she told herself. Why would Dez take the cookie jar? He'd just said himself that he saw no reason anybody would want it. Of course, that could be an attempt to cover up, but the fact was the man had just about as much sentimental feeling as the jar itself was capable of experiencing. And in any case, he couldn't possibly have known that she wouldn't unpack the box the moment he set it down and discover the jar missing.

Of course he hadn't taken it. This sudden attack of suspicion was only her own guilty conscience running amok, trying desperately to shift the blame to an innocent party. Anyone but herself.

That realization only made her feel guiltier yet. Suddenly she couldn't stand it anymore, and the tears she'd been holding back with such effort overflowed.

Dez put an arm around her shoulders, which only made

her cry harder. If he knew she'd been suspicious of him, even for a moment, he wouldn't be trying to comfort her.

He handed her a tissue from the box on her desk. "We'll fix it, sweetheart."

She couldn't stop sobbing. "I don't know how you think this can be fixed," she managed to say. "Anyway, it's not just the cookie jar. I'm trying to take good care of Essie's legacy. I don't just want to keep her museum going, I want to make it great. But instead I go and lose her cookie jar!"

"You'll make the museum great, Gina. Let's talk about that proposition you offered me."

"Trading the Tyler-Royale building for Essie's house?" Gina blotted her eyes. "What about it?"

"I've been considering it. I think we can make some kind of a deal."

She stared at him and then burst into tears all over again. "You know perfectly well this museum can't afford that whole building. You've been telling me that all along, and you're right. So if you think you're doing me any favors now—"

"Gina, we will work out a solution. Just stop crying so we can talk about it, all right?"

Suddenly what he'd said hit her, hard. The man who didn't even like old buildings was suddenly going out of his way and making an enormous financial sacrifice so she could have what she wanted?

Only so he can have Essie's house in return, whispered a voice in the back of her mind.

But wanting the house wasn't enough to explain this willingness to deal, she thought. In fact, there was only one explanation. The man who had never before found an old building worth saving had changed in some essential way.

She'd known from the moment she met him that he was

unusual, one of a kind. He'd always been special. Now…now he was extraordinary.

It was no wonder she'd fallen in love with him.

Oh, no, she thought. *What a foolish thing to do.*

At least Gina had stopped crying, Dez thought. She looked dazed, almost as if he'd picked up the rusty old miner's shovel which was leaning against her desk—why was it standing there, anyway?—and hit her over the head with it, but she wasn't sobbing wildly anymore.

Was she honestly so flabbergasted by what he'd said that she couldn't even talk? That wasn't very flattering, but it was probably true.

He had to admit, though, that nothing about this conversation was going the way he'd expected. He'd just been working up to introduce the subject when the damn cookie jar had turned up missing. Who'd have thought a cookie jar could cause so much trouble?

He sat down on the corner of her desk. "I'll make sure you get a suitable building."

She blinked, and frowned. "Not Tyler-Royale?"

"Gina, for heaven's sake, you yelled at me just now when you thought that's what I was offering you."

"Oh. I guess I did. So what are you offering? Because if you've still got St. Francis Church on the brain—"

"I don't," he said hastily. "As a matter of fact, I've got plans for it, so it's completely out of the equation. Can we shake hands on the deal?"

"Are you joking? Without knowing what you're offering to trade?"

Dez sighed. "There's no shortage of buildings in this town. There are some warehouses down by the lake that would be—"

"Maybe," she said warily. "But I'm not agreeing to give up Essie's house for an unknown."

"Unknown right at the moment, maybe—but it's guaranteed to be better than what you've got now."

"By whose standards? Yours or mine?"

It hadn't taken her long to pull herself together, Dez thought irritably. "All right. I'll find you a building, you look at it, and then we'll deal."

He didn't wait for an answer, because he was already running behind schedule.

And because now—no matter what it took to get it—he absolutely must have Essie's house.

Gina was still in shock. She had only a vague idea of what she'd said to Dez, because the sudden realization that she'd been idiot enough to fall in love with him was still echoing 'round her brain even after he was gone.

She supposed she should have seen it coming. But from the first moment everything about their relationship had been so off kilter that there had been no reason to be cautious. She couldn't possibly be seriously attracted to a guy whose values were so different from her own.

Play games with him, yes. Flirt, definitely. But get serious about him? Fall in love? Not a chance.

Except that was exactly what she'd done.

He had knocked her off guard because he'd turned out to be so very different from what she'd thought he was. Somehow, seeing Essie's house again had been a turning point for him. Something about it had awakened a sense of history, of destiny, of family, that had lain dormant inside Dez so long that he—and everybody around him—had thought it was dead.

That hidden inner self was the part of him that Gina had seen, without even being fully aware of what she was looking at. That was the part she had fallen in love with, the Dez who could care about Essie's house as much as she did.

But now what? Getting serious had never been part of the bargain, but now that she'd gone and done it anyway…how would Dez react to that?

What would happen if next time she saw him, she were to stroll up, lay one hand on his lapel, and say, "By the way, Dez, I love you?"

He'd probably think she was making some kind of bizarre joke. That would be bad enough. But if he took her seriously—that would be even worse. He'd either turn pale, or he'd scream and run—in much the same way she would have done yesterday, if he had come up to her, put his hand on her shoulder, and said, "You know, Gina, I think I love you."

She could almost hear him, and that was even more painful. Because she knew how the words would sound—and because she knew she would never hear him say them.

The village fair had gotten off to an incredible start. Gina wandered through the booths and tents, trying to keep an eye on everything at once. Some of her volunteers, in historic costumes, were portraying early settlers and showing off long-ago skills like butter-churning to the delight of the small children who were watching.

It was too bad, she thought, that nobody had asked Dez to play Desmond Kerrigan. He'd have been a natural as the host of the house, welcoming a throng of guests. Of course, he'd been a little busy lately—probably too busy to study a part and be fitted for a costume.

Gina hadn't even seen him since the day the cookie jar had vanished—disappeared right along with her illusions of being aloof and uninterested in him.

She hadn't yet recovered from either shock. The police had not been hopeful about the chances of recovering the pottery jar. And though she'd tried to convince herself that her sudden realization had been only a mistake after all, a few days spent away from Dez had not helped. She missed being teased. She missed his kissing lessons. She even missed the blunt way he challenged her beliefs and sometimes forced her to change her mind.

She missed *him*. All of him.

She'd expected that he would come to the village fair— he had, after all, bought a ticket. But as the evening wore on and the sky darkened to indigo, her hopes diminished to wistful dreams.

She tried to tell herself that he was simply busy—trying to find her a satisfactory building, perhaps. But she couldn't quite make herself believe it. Instead, she was afraid that somehow she had given herself away. Somehow she had let him guess what she was feeling.

And she suspected that Dez, realizing how she felt about him but unable to return her affection, was staying as far away as he could. Perhaps he was doing the kindest thing he could think of by keeping his distance. Or perhaps, she admitted, the explanation was less selfless, and he was protecting himself in the best way he knew....

She was thinking about that as she waited in line at the homemade-ice-cream stand. She'd put off sampling any of the treats, telling herself she was too busy with the workings of the fair to indulge in homemade taffy or funnel cakes or kettle corn. In fact, what she'd been doing was waiting for Dez to come, because there wasn't a single treat at the fair she wouldn't enjoy more if she was in his company.

It had been foolish of her, of course. He wasn't coming, and it was time for her to move on. She'd had a lesson, that was all. She'd get over it eventually. She'd get over him. In the meantime, the first step was to go on just as normal and pretend that everything was all right.

She waited to be last in line. It was simple good manners, she told herself, to take care of guests before herself. It wasn't like she was still waiting for…anybody.

When it was her turn she stepped up to the makeshift counter. "Strawberry, if you still have it," she said.

Beside her, Dez said, "Make it two."

Gina spun to face him. "You came. You're here!" she said, before she could stop herself.

For a few seconds, he looked into her eyes, and then he turned to the man behind the counter to trade a folded bill for two old-fashioned soda fountain dishes heaped with pale pink ice cream.

Gina gritted her teeth. *Fool,* she told herself, and deliberately smothered her feelings, trying to tamp down her joy until it appeared to be nothing more than the pleasure she'd shown when greeting any other guest. "I'm glad you could make it after all," she said as he handed her a dish. She was quite proud; her voice sounded perfectly normal. Friendly, warm, but not excited. "It would have been such a shame to waste your ticket. To say nothing of the hazelnut coffee we ordered just for you."

"And to miss out on Essie's garden gate being open for the first time in who knows how many years," he agreed. "Would you rather sit down or walk around?"

Gina considered. Sitting down meant talking, and looking at each other. Normally it was a prospect she would have welcomed. But tonight, when she would have to put forth every iota of self-control to stay on her guard… "Walk around," she said. "You haven't seen any of the fair yet."

"Oh, I've been here for a while."

She could have kicked herself for assuming that he would come in the gate and straight to her. Why should he have rushed to her side? Why would she have expected him to? She only hoped those questions didn't occur to him.

She went on hastily, "We've had a lot of last-minute ticket sales. That's unusual, for an event like this. Usually everyone who's interested buys in advance. We should turn a nice profit."

You're babbling, Gina. Shut up. Or at least change the subject. "Thank you for the ice cream."

"You're welcome. I see what you mean about the crowd. Essie's garden hasn't held this many people since old Desmond's gardeners planted it."

He hadn't seized the chance for a kissing lesson. For that matter, he hadn't even touched her. And after that one long look, he'd seemed to be more interested in everything—anything—else.

Sadness washed over Gina. *Don't think about it now,* she ordered herself.

"You must have been working hard."

He shot a sideways look at her.

She added hastily, "At least I assume you have, because you haven't been around to show me a building yet."

"It's been harder to find a suitable one than I expected."

"That's good. I mean, if you're being choosy it'll save me a lot of time." Of course, she reflected sadly, it also meant that he wouldn't have to spend time with her, taking her around to inspect all the possibilities.

"The garden looks better at night," Dez mused. "Or maybe it's actually been improved by being trampled by the crowd."

"All the people haven't hurt anything. The grass will look tired tomorrow, but the plants will still be fine." She reached up to touch the glossy leaf of a holly bush. "It could still be beautiful, you know. Everything's here—it's just overgrown."

He looked as if he had serious doubts about that. Gina didn't push the subject. It wasn't up to her to say what he should do with the garden.

They wandered between the rows of booths, but they hadn't covered anywhere near all the fair when closing time came. Before long, the grounds were almost empty; only the volunteers who had helped to set up and run the booths remained.

Gina helped to clear up the ice cream booth, while Dez lent a hand to take down tables. Finally the mess was cleared away. "I'll give you a ride home," Dez said.

"Oh—that's not necessary." Gina fumbled for an excuse. "I think I'll stay awhile and total up the ticket sales and everything."

Eleanor, passing by with a tray full of ice cream dishes, said, "Oh, for heaven's sake, Gina, go home. You've been here long enough for one day."

"So have you," Gina called after her, but Eleanor didn't stop. "Thanks," Gina said. "I'd appreciate a ride."

She knew she was too quiet on the drive. Unusually quiet. She just hoped he would chalk it up to exhaustion instead of looking for other reasons. In front of the row house, she said, "Thank you," and started to get out.

"I'm coming in," Dez said.

Her heart skipped a beat. Why? What did he want to say to her that couldn't have been said at the fair? *I'm not going to like this,* she thought. But whatever it was, perhaps it was better to get it over with—now, privately.

Whatever it was.

Mrs. Mason must have gone on vacation, for she wasn't peeking through her door as they climbed the stairs. Gina fumbled with her key, and Dez took it out of her hand, turned the lock, and opened the door. She stepped inside, but before she could turn on the lights he caught her hand and pulled her toward him. Gently, he cupped his hands around her face and kissed her, long and hard. And then, without breaking the kiss, he slid his hands along her throat, over her shoulders, and down her back, until she was held fast in his arms, molded against the length of his body.

If she had wanted to, Gina couldn't have resisted that tender assault on her senses. And she didn't want to. She wanted to stay there forever, sheltered in his arms, feeling treasured, feeling precious.

Even when he raised his head, he didn't release her. It was just as well, for Gina wasn't sure she could stand on her own. She looked up at him, her vision foggy, and said, "What—"

"You gave yourself away," Dez said.

She was stunned. If he knew how she felt...and this was his reaction....

"You were happy to see me," he whispered, and kissed her again, softly this time.

So he didn't know all of her secret. A bit of her inner glow dissipated, but so did a good deal of the fear she'd been feeling. So long as she was careful...

"Was that lesson three?" she asked. Her voice felt as if she hadn't used it in a long time.

"Yes. Intended to demonstrate the power of restraint."

"*That* was restrained?"

"I wanted to kiss you at the fair. See how much waiting improves the final result? Just holding back a while... resisting desire..."

"But..." She hardly recognized her voice. "What if I don't feel like holding back? Or resisting? Or waiting?"

''That's lesson four,'' he whispered against her lips. ''Total abandon. But that one's up to you.''

For a split second, she hesitated, and then she closed her eyes and kissed him. It felt just a little like stepping out of an airplane without checking to make sure she had a parachute. But when his arms tightened around her, Gina knew that no matter how wild the turbulence, he would not let her plunge out of control.

She had never let herself dream about what it would be like to make love with him, for it had seemed to her that the fantasy would provide only needless pain. Now she knew that fantasizing would have been not only painful but futile—for the soul-shattering joy of joining with him was outside her power to imagine.

Gina sat up in bed with the coffee Dez had brought her, watching him get dressed. Despite the fact that his clothes had spent the night on her bedroom floor, he looked crisp, fresh, and bright-eyed. Only the shadow of beard gave him away.

He looked delicious.

He settled the collar of his shirt and sat down on the edge of the bed, leaning over to kiss her. Gina's heart gave a little skip of pure joy, and she had to remind herself that caution was still the order of the day. *Act casual,* she told herself. *Not as if your world has settled into an entirely new orbit. Even though it has.* ''Are you off to find me a building this morning?'' she teased.

''Nope.''

She was puzzled. ''But I thought— Weren't you looking?''

''Oh, yes. You were right, you know—up to a point. The best place for your museum is Tyler-Royale. But I was also right—you can't handle all of it. So here's the deal—you get one floor of the building for the museum. It's easily ten times the floor space you have here, and since it's all open you'll have all the flexibility you could ask for. It'll be easier to secure, easier to—''

She flung herself at him. ''You're going to save it!''

''Yeah, I guess I am,'' he admitted. He sounded almost ashamed of himself, Gina thought. ''I was going to tell you that last night, but you seemed to have other priorities.''

She could feel herself turning pink.

He laughed and kissed her again. ''You were right about the building too, as it turns out. The darn thing is so solid it would be practically impossible to knock it down.''

Gina knew better. If he wanted to, Dez could knock anything down. It was because of her that he was saving the building. ''And the rest of it?''

''The plans call for the museum to be on the second floor with shops at street level and the upper floors turned into luxury condos.''

She couldn't have asked for more. ''Thank you,'' she whispered, and drew him close for a long kiss.

''Hold that thought,'' he said. ''I'd collect right now if I didn't have architects and engineers waiting for me.''

''I hate architects and engineers.''

''So do I, honey,'' he said softly. ''So do I.''

Everything she looked at had a sort of pink halo around it. Even the hole in the exhibit left by the still-missing cookie jar, though it dragged down Gina's spirits, couldn't ruin her day. The fair had been a success, the pledges were still coming in from her stint in the hot tub, the museum would shortly have a new home... And she had Dez.

Hold it right there, she warned herself. Spending the night with her was hardly a lifetime commitment. But she knew it was more than a casual fling for Dez, too. And maybe someday, after the museum had moved, they could work together on restoring Essie's house to the grandeur it had once possessed.

She was in the living room, visualizing the blocked-off windows once more open and draped in Victorian velvet, when Nathan Haynes came in. "Ms. Haskell," he said. "I'm sorry I haven't had a chance to talk to you earlier about the house. I'll still write a full report for the board of directors, of course, but would you like a preview of my findings now?"

"Not really," she said happily. "It doesn't matter much, though I'm sure the board will be interested. The one who might like to hear the details is Dez. Since he'll be the one doing the renovations—"

"Renovations?" he said slowly. "I'm afraid I don't quite understand."

"Oh, I don't suppose anyone has told you. There are still some loose ends to tie up, and the board has to give its approval, so keep this under your hat for a while, all right? We're going to do a trade—Dez is getting Essie's house back into the family, and the museum will move into the—"

The architect was shaking his head. "Dez isn't planning to renovate this house."

And how would you know? "You must have misunderstood, Mr. Haynes."

"No, Ms. Haskell. I've been drawing the plans for what will be built on this site. Just as soon as the museum has moved out, the house will come down."

"No," she whispered.

"We'll do the project in stages, of course. Some of the renovation on Tyler-Royale will be first, so the museum can move. Then we'll clear this site, from here all the way through St. Francis Church, including the building where his office is.''

''No!'' But if it wasn't true, how did he know where the museum was to move?

His eyes held understanding and sympathy. ''This lot is one of the key corners, as an anchor for the apartment development he's going to put up. He'd been planning a single tower, but having this site means the project can be three times the size—'' He seemed to realize she wasn't listening. ''If there's anything particular you want from the house, Ms. Haskell—newel posts, paneling, front door, plants from the garden, I don't know what it might be— just make a list. Maybe there'll be time to do a little salvage before the bulldozers move in, though it depends on the rest of the construction schedule.''

That was what made her really believe that he knew what he was talking about—the cool, clipped offer to try to save the newel post, with no promises that he would succeed. Obviously, she thought, he'd worked with Dez before.

Nathan Haynes was telling her the truth.

Dez wanted Essie's house all right. He wanted it desperately. But not so he could live in it. Not so he could treasure it.

He wanted it only so he could destroy it.

CHAPTER TEN

GINA had won, in a way. The Tyler-Royale building would be saved.

But she had also lost, and the defeat weighed far more heavily than the victory. The price she had paid to save one building was not simply the destruction of a second one. That kind of trade might perhaps be palatable, in some circumstances. But not here. Not now.

It was the knowledge that she had betrayed Essie's trust which haunted Gina. Essie had believed in her. Essie had had faith that no matter what, Gina would remain true to the cause—to Essie's cause, and Essie's museum.

And Gina had tried, there was no doubt about that. She had made what she thought were the right choices—the choices she believed Essie herself would have made.

But she'd been dead wrong. In her innocence, she had trusted Dez...

No, she admitted, that wasn't quite correct. It hadn't been pure innocence which had made her put her faith in him and believe that he would act the way she wanted him to. In her love-fogged state, she had deliberately blinded herself.

She had known his history. She had known his feelings. Heaven knew he'd made no effort to hide his attitude—even Essie had known that Dez was about as far from being a conservationist as a man could possibly be. Even harder to bear was the memory of Essie telling her, in essence, that Dez lived to knock down buildings.

But Gina had wanted to believe that she was important

enough to him that he would change. That he would not only make an effort to understand her point of view, but that he would then, inevitably, agree with her.

And, it had seemed, she was right. He was going to save the Tyler-Royale building.

But only because it was convenient for him. Only because letting it stand cleared the way for an even bigger project.

"And they all lived happily ever after," she said under her breath. What a fairy tale she had constructed for herself!

"I'm sorry," Nathan Haynes said tentatively. "If you'd like me to explain—"

Gina shook her head and turned away. How could he possibly expect her to stand there calmly while he described how the bulldozers and wrecking balls would turn Essie's house to dust so Dez could build a set of cookie-cutter towers?

She could hardly breathe with the weight of pain, of responsibility, which had suddenly descended on her. Essie had trusted her...

That was bad enough by itself. But in truth there was an even harsher price to pay than the knowledge that she had naively double-crossed her benefactor. Gina had betrayed herself.

She had been absolutely wrong about Dez. She had fallen in love with a fantasy. She had created the man she wanted him to be, and then she had let herself tumble head over heels in love with the illusion she herself had manufactured.

Now she didn't even know anymore what was real. She only knew what wasn't.

At first, Gina had half expected Dez to turn up at any time. But as the minutes, and then the hours, ticked by with infinite slowness, she realized he wasn't going to appear soon—and perhaps he didn't intend to come at all.

Dez was no doubt busy, probably putting the finishing touches on the plans for the new tower which would replace Essie's house—and from what Nathan Haynes had said, a good deal of the rest of the neighborhood too. Gina didn't remember the details, because she'd been too shocked by the bombshell he'd dropped to pay close attention. But hadn't Nathan Haynes said something about St. Francis Church disappearing as well? That was three long blocks away from Essie's house, so it was no small project they were talking about.

If Dez hadn't had architects and engineers waiting for him, he'd told her that morning, he would have stayed with her. That alone, she thought bitterly, should have warned her of what was going on—and also told her how very low she ranked on his list. If it had been convenient for him, he'd have no doubt enjoyed staying in her bed a little longer. But faced with the choice between her and a bunch of engineers and architects...

Perhaps that wasn't entirely fair, she thought. Keeping people waiting while he indulged himself wasn't exactly the way to make a business successful.

But no matter how true that observation was, it didn't make her feel any less resentful. Didn't he even care how she felt about all this? Was he just waiting a while in the hope that she'd cool off? If so, it was foolish of him to think that a little time would make a difference in how she felt. Or—now that he had achieved everything he wanted—didn't he intend to come back to her at all?

Or perhaps she was still assuming too much—believing that she was important enough for him to even worry about. Why should he rush over to the museum to find her so he could explain himself? The odds were that Nathan Haynes hadn't made a big thing of telling Dez about her reaction. He might not have said anything at all.

And even if he had mentioned it, she admitted to herself, why would Dez have given the whole thing a second thought? After last night, why would he be concerned? He must think he had Gina exactly where he wanted her—in a tight corner with the wool pulled over her eyes.

She'd certainly behaved last night as if she wanted him desperately enough not to object, no matter what he did. So why would he expect to meet trouble today?

If he bothered to show up at all. She hadn't paid much attention at the time—but when he'd left her apartment this morning, he hadn't exactly made any arrangements. Not even so much as a dinner date...

As a matter of fact, she heard him before she saw him. It was late afternoon and Gina was sitting at her desk at the top of the attic stairs, paying the museum's bills, when she heard his voice and Eleanor's near the door at the bottom of the staircase.

Though Gina couldn't distinguish the words, there was no mistaking the sound of Dez's voice. Even the first few times she'd heard him speak, back when she hadn't much liked a single thing he'd said to her, she'd had to admit that his voice was rich and warm as well as arrogant.

Then he spoke a little louder. "Here," he said. "You take care of this, and I'll get her."

Gina's fingers tightened on her pencil as footsteps started up. She bent her head over the locksmith's bill.

She expected that he'd stop at the top of the stairs, if only to check out the atmosphere. If Nathan Haynes hadn't warned him of the storm clouds surrounding the museum, surely Eleanor had.

But without a pause he came around the desk to stand beside her, reaching out one hand as if he intended to curve his fingers around the nape of her neck. She saw the move from the corner of her eye and almost as a reflex action, Gina pushed back her chair, sliding as far away from him as she could go. The wheel of her chair thudded against the base of the hall tree next to her desk.

He stood still. "Nate told me you seemed upset."

"Perceptive of him." Gina didn't look up from the bill she was still holding. "Ridiculous, what a locksmith charges to unstick one small rusted-shut garden gate."

Dez perched on the corner of her desk. "Want to tell me about it, Gina?"

The dull buzz of anger which had been humming in her ears since Nathan Haynes's announcement grew even louder. "If you think I'm going to explain it to you, you're dead wrong. As far as that goes, if you actually need it explained, you're in worse shape than I thought." She tossed the locksmith's bill onto the pile on her desk blotter. "The deal's off, Dez. No trade."

"You can't do that."

"Watch me."

"You can't make a decision like that without your board's approval."

"No, I can't," she admitted. "But then, I can't exactly agree to the deal without consulting them, either. Careless of you not to get things in writing first—because since the board hasn't signed off on the trade yet, all I have to do is recommend against the move."

"And they'll override you in a minute, once they've read Nate Haynes's report."

"Why?" Gina countered. "What's going to be in his report? And how much did you have to pay him in order to get it to say exactly what you wanted?"

He slid off the desk, landing with a thump that shook

the attic floor. "Dammit, Gina, you can't say things like that."

"Oh, don't waste your breath. I'll say what I want to about you."

"You can talk about me all you want, but don't go around accusing Nate of taking bribes. He doesn't operate that way."

"And how do you know he doesn't? Because you've tried to bribe him? Stop trying to distract me, Dez. What's going to be in his report that will convince my board to give you this house, even after I tell them Nathan Haynes is actually working for you instead of them?"

"The truth."

"You expect me to believe that, when you've already lied to me?"

"How?" He paced across the attic and back to her desk. "By promising to save Essie's house and restore it to glory? Your problem is, you can't make that accusation stick, Gina—because I never promised anything of the sort."

"You certainly implied it."

"No, I didn't. You assumed it—because that was what you wanted to happen. In fact, you wanted it so badly that you did a sell job on yourself."

Gina thought about it. Was it possible he was right—that even with no evidence, she had persuaded herself that he intended to do what she wanted him to?

Why not? she asked herself wearily. She'd managed to convince herself that he cared about her feelings. That he cared about her. Of course she'd have had no trouble convincing herself about a little thing like renovating a house.

"You never once asked me what I was going to do with this house, Gina."

No, she admitted. She hadn't ever asked. So perhaps he

hadn't actually lied—but he certainly hadn't told the truth, either. Instead, he had deliberately used her assumption to his own advantage. "You should have told me anyway. Warned me."

"I tried," he said. "But you refused to hear what I was saying."

Gina was no longer listening. It felt as if something had broken inside her, releasing a torrent that she had held back too long. "You knew how I felt about this house—how I felt about Essie—and you deliberately used that to get your way. You know perfectly well if you'd told me you intended to tear it down, I'd have thrown you out. So you didn't tell me."

"I *didn't* intend to tear it down. Not at first. I didn't even want the thing—you're the one who insisted I must have this overwhelming longing to own it."

That stopped her cold for a moment.

"You're what started me thinking about building in this end of town in the first place, Gina. If it hadn't been for you, I'd never have owned St. Francis Church in the first place—I only bought it because I thought it would get you off my back."

"Oh, thanks—dump the responsibility on me!"

"I was trying to give you credit for a damned fine idea. When you first suggested I build on the St. Francis site, I thought you were crazy. But the longer I looked at it, the more sense it made. Building here means the whole neighborhood will come back into style. You won't be able to afford to live in your row house anymore, because people will be standing in line to turn those buildings back into single-family homes."

"That's supposed to make me feel better? Tear down something else if you have to, but—"

"You're actually going to give me permission to demolish anything at all? How gracious of you."

"Just don't wreck Essie's house!"

"Gina, it's only a house. I'm tearing down the building where my office is, too."

She was aghast that he would compare the two. "Do you expect me to believe you're going to shed tears over that? You told me you'd keep that building just as long as it served your purpose—and no longer. So what if its time is up? This house is different."

"What in the hell is so important about it?"

He won't understand. He can't understand. It's useless to tell him.

And yet…something inside her whispered that she must not hold back anything which might make a difference.

Gina took a deep breath. "Essie was everything to me, Dez." She wet her lips and whispered what she had never said out loud to anyone before, not even to Essie. "She saved me."

"Fine. Essie was special. That doesn't explain why the house—"

"I would do anything—*anything!*—to protect her legacy. I told you she gave me a job. What I didn't tell you was why." Gina rubbed her eyes. "My parents died when I was four. I barely remember them. By the time I was thirteen I'd lived in at least a dozen foster homes. The one I was in right then was all right, I guess, though my foster parents were mostly interested in the money they got to take care of me. I don't know what they did with it all—though I suppose it wasn't really all that much. It just seemed a fortune to me at the time."

"You mean, they didn't spend it on you, as they were supposed to."

"No, they didn't. I needed a pair of shoes—mine had a

big crack across the bottom of the soles, and it was the middle of winter and my feet were wet and cold…'' Her voice dwindled. ''They said the money was gone and I'd have to do without till the next check came. So I just took the shoes. From Tyler-Royale, as a matter of fact.''

He sighed. ''And you were caught, of course.''

''Essie's the one who caught me. She was trying on a pair of those ghastly, heavy, black clodhoppers she always wore. The store must have special-ordered them for her, because surely nobody else would have thought of wearing them. Anyway, I didn't see her when I went in, but I was in one of her history classes that term, so she noticed me.''

''I see. It's a good thing Essie was the one who saw you, instead of someone from the store.''

''I wouldn't put it quite that way,'' Gina said dryly. ''When I stuffed the shoes under my coat, she grabbed me by the collar and—still in her stocking feet—hauled me straight upstairs to the manager of the store, and he called the police.''

She shot a sideways look at him. Dez looked horrified. By the crime, she wondered, or by the harshness of the reaction? Not that it mattered what he thought of her. Not now.

She couldn't stop now, that was sure. ''When the judge told me he was going to send me to reform school—''

''For taking a pair of shoes you desperately needed?''

Gina looked him straight in the eye. ''It wasn't the first time I'd shoplifted. And what I took wasn't always—strictly speaking—something I needed. It hadn't taken Essie any time at all to figure that out. But as I was standing there in front of the judge, literally shaking in fear, she stood up in the back of the courtroom and told the judge she would take responsibility for me.''

''Shock treatment,'' Dez murmured.

"She gave me a job dusting all of her treasures, and I paid for the shoes out of my first wages."

"No wonder you feel you owe her."

"Not for keeping me out of reform school, actually," Gina mused. "There were days I'd have rather been there than in middle school in Lakemont."

"Because of people like Jennifer Carleton, I suppose."

Gina nodded. "You have no idea how cruel thirteen-year-old girls can be to someone who doesn't quite fit in. Someone who looks like the teacher's pet, even though Essie never once took it easy on me in history class. No—though it seems backward, it wasn't keeping me out of the juvenile justice system that I really appreciated. It was everything else she did for me." She wouldn't have been surprised if he'd looked impatient, but he didn't seem to be. So she went on. "Essie soon realized I had no clue about manners, or etiquette, or for that matter even posture. Would you believe she's the one who taught me how to buy clothes?"

His gaze summed up the smart cut of her skirt, the fit of her sweater, and he said flatly, "Not in a million years."

"Well, she did. She may have only worn shapeless black herself, but she knew style when she saw it. It reached the point where I almost lived here. And sometimes…" Her voice dropped almost to a whisper as she confessed, "Sometimes I'd pretend that Essie was really my aunt. That Desmond Kerrigan had been my great-grandfather. That I had a past. A family history. And before I knew it…"

"You were hooked. That's why everything she loved is so important to you."

"Yes. Essie's the reason I ended up in college instead of jail. She's the only reason I'm here." She bit her lip and looked straight at him, desperate for him to understand. "It was one thing to move the museum away from here when

I knew—at least I thought I knew—that the house would be restored. But to have it destroyed... Dez, please don't take this away from me. Don't make me break my promise to Essie.''

There was a long silence. "I wish I could give you what you want, sweetheart.''

The heaviness in his voice tore away the last shred of hope. Gina began to cry, though she was almost unaware of the slow tears burning painful streaks down her face because every nerve and bone and sinew in her body hurt too. It had all been in vain—exposing her sordid secrets, sharing the deepest convictions of her soul.

"Gina," he said slowly, "you aren't breaking your promise to Essie if it's impossible for you to keep it.''

She wiped her cheek. "You expect me to forgive myself because you're the one who's making it impossible? If I'd only minded my own business in the first place, kept my mouth shut about Tyler-Royale and St. Francis Church, everything would be all right.''

"Not exactly." He reached out and his fingers clasped 'round her wrist. "Come with me. There's something I need to show you.''

She tried without success to shake off his grip. "No. Just leave me alone, Dez. I can't take any more of this. I can't stand to love somebody who—" The words were out before she could stop herself.

Horrified by what she had admitted, Gina looked down at his long, tanned fingers, still clasped around her wrist. She wouldn't blame him if, after that artless admission, he pulled back from her as if he'd suddenly touched a hot coal—or realized that he'd reached into a nest of vipers.

Instead, his grip tightened. "Too bad," he said coolly. "You're coming. I'd rather not carry you down those stairs, but if I have to—"

"Why won't you leave me alone?" she pleaded. "Just let me sit here."

"Because you need to see Nate's report. Or, rather, the evidence it's based on." He tugged at her hand, and unable to resist any longer, Gina stood up. She felt shaky, and it seemed that the stairs creaked more than usual under her feet.

He didn't let go of her until they were in the kitchen, and even then it was only to point up at the ceiling. "Tell me that crack isn't worse than it was a couple of weeks ago."

"It looks the same to me. Why?"

"Remember it." He unlocked the door to the basement, so nearly hidden in the shadow of the big old refrigerator that Gina had almost forgotten it was there. She pulled back from the dark, yawning descent.

Dez pulled a penlight from his pocket. "How long has it been since you've been down here?"

"I don't remember. The last time I brought something up for the camera display, I suppose."

"Watch your head." He went first, ducking under the low beam at the top of the stairs. At the bottom, he waited till she caught up, then played the penlight over the beams above their heads as if he was looking for something. "There—see the split in that beam? It goes all the way through."

"Is that why there's a crack in the kitchen?"

"No—the beam is the reason there's so much dust in the closet under the main stairway. The support under the stairs is weakened, so the steps vibrate every time someone goes up and down, and bits of plaster shake loose."

How would he know whether there was dust in the closets? Because, Gina recalled, when she'd pulled out the box of tickets for the village fair in order to sell him one, she'd had to wipe off the top of it. As a matter of fact, she thought, lately Eleanor seemed to be always dusting. But Gina hadn't paid much attention. She'd assumed it was because of something outside—the weather, or wind-borne dirt, even construction going on nearby—or because of the increased number of visitors going in and out. It hadn't occurred to her that the problem might be in the house itself.

"The kitchen is cracked," Dez went on relentlessly, "because the foundation on that side of the house has sagged. Come over here." He led her around the base of the stairs, past a stack of wooden crates, and played the flashlight over a stone wall.

It looked damp, though she'd never noticed that before. And was it only the power of suggestion or was the center of the wall really bulging inward?

"If you had tried to excavate in the garden to dig footings for a new wing, you'd have buckled the whole wall. Good thing you didn't put the tents for the village fair right up against the house—just driving the stakes could have been enough to make that wall collapse."

Gina could feel the blood draining from her face as the truth dawned.

Dez turned the penlight toward her. "Want me to go on? That's the worst of it down here, but maybe you should take a look at the vines on the back of the house. They've chewed into the mortar till some of the bricks are actually loose. And then there's the question of dry rot in the sills—"

"No," Gina said. "Stop. I don't need to hear any more." She put her fingertips to her temples. "And I've been letting school children run up and down and bounce on the stairs…"

"Nate says the building is in no immediate danger of collapse. But the bottom line is that it's past saving."

"Why didn't you tell me?" She was having trouble getting a full breath.

"Come on," he said. "Let's go back upstairs before we choke on the musty smell."

He stood back to let her go first. Gina almost had to drag herself up the steps, until Dez put a helpful hand on her hip. The reminder of intimacy jolted her, and she hurried the rest of the way.

He closed the door. "How about something cold to drink, to cut the taste of that basement?"

Gina shook her head. "Help yourself."

He reached into the refrigerator and grabbed a can, seemingly at random. Popping the top, he leaned against the refrigerator. "Why didn't I tell you the details? Mostly because I didn't know the worst of it myself till I talked to Nate just this morning. But I did try to warn you, Gina. I told you the place was falling in around you. It's a hundred and fifty years old, and it hasn't had any significant maintenance for a century."

She shook her head. "I thought you were just—"

"Being my usual destructive self?"

"Yes," she admitted. "But I should have known you wouldn't..."

She stopped. Was she doing it all over again? Convincing herself that he'd really wanted to save the house, that he would have done it if it were possible?

Dez sighed. "Much as I like being your knight in shining armor, I have to be honest, Gina."

"You wouldn't have saved it, no matter what." At least he'd admitted it, her heart argued. At least he was telling her the truth rather than saying what she wanted to hear.

As if it matters to him what I think.

She pulled a chair away from the kitchen table and sat down.

Dez nodded, almost sadly. "Even if it was in a lot better shape than it is, I'd still want to tear it down."

Want to. Was there just a hint of hope there? *You're a fool,* she told herself. She was still clinging to the last fragment of her dream, even when common sense said there was nothing left to dream about.

"Though you could probably have persuaded me to move it. Anyway, it doesn't signify. Honey, Essie wouldn't expect you to try to save the unsalvageable."

Gina bit her lip. He sounded absolutely certain, and she wanted so badly to believe him. But... "How can you be so sure of that? You barely knew her."

"Because you just told me everything that was important about her," he said softly. "The woman who grabbed you by the collar, who stood silent while you were questioned by the police, who let you shake in fear in front of a judge—that woman was no misty-eyed visionary, Gina. She was a practical, no-nonsense, get-the-job-done type."

Reluctantly, she admitted, "That's true. Whatever it took, Essie did it."

"She knew that sympathy was no way to straighten you out, so she did what was necessary. And she would do the same this time. She wouldn't be happy about the house— but she wouldn't waste time fighting circumstances either."

"As I have, you mean?"

"No, that's not what I mean." He sounded impatient. "Gina, your devotion is understandable. It's admirable. But I don't think Essie expected you to follow blindly in her path. I don't think she'd have wanted you to. She put her faith in you because she believed you could be your own woman. Make your own decisions. Reach your own judgments. In fact, I think she would have been annoyed as hell to see you stuck in the past.''

Gina was stung. "Stuck—!"

"Yes, stuck," he said relentlessly. "Treasuring history, protecting it, is fine. But—"

"Oh, that's pretty hilarious, coming from you." She pushed her chair back and started for the door.

He stepped into her path. "If she'd wanted you to be her clone, Gina, she wouldn't have taught you how to buy clothes in anything but shapeless black.''

The statement was so ridiculous that she stopped and stared at him. His eyes were the shimmering green of emeralds. He was laughing at her.

No...he was laughing *with* her. It was an entirely different thing.

"Essie isn't in these bricks, Gina," he said, suddenly serious again. "She's inside you. She always will be."

I'm sorry, Essie. It seemed to Gina that the house sighed in answer—not in approval, exactly, but in acceptance— and a tight knot deep inside her slowly relaxed.

Gina took a deep breath and nodded. "All right. I surrender."

"I don't want you to surrender. I want you to agree."

"Funny," she mused. "That sounds familiar. Okay—I agree. Now what?" She looked around, her eyes almost misty. "Nathan Haynes said if there was anything I wanted to salvage, to let him know and he'd try."

"Absolutely. We'll keep all the pieces we possibly can."

She shook her head. "That's sweet, but even with an entire floor to house the museum, we won't have room for everything." Sadness surged through her at the idea.

"If you want some mementos for the museum so you can put up an exhibit about its first home, that's fine with me. But that wasn't what I had in mind."

Gina frowned.

"I thought maybe we'd design one of those luxury condos in the Tyler-Royale building for us." He shot a glance at her and then looked quickly away. "It would be even handier for you to get to work than it is now. And you'll be spending even more time on the museum, I suppose—at least at first. But with the shops and the condos providing a steady income, you can actually pay a staff instead of relying so heavily on volunteers. Once that's all set up, maybe you can take it easier. Have some time for other things."

She stared at him. "I... Dez, be serious. You can't mean you'd actually give the rents from the whole building to the museum."

He began to laugh. "Gina, you are incredible—you're actually more concerned about the museum's budget than the fact that I just proposed to you. Damn, maybe you *are* Essie's clone."

Her throat felt as if she'd swallowed a roll of cotton. "You just...what?" she said faintly.

"I was trying to say that if you can stand having me around, I want to spend my life with you." He set his soda can down. "Come here."

She didn't move.

The silence stretched out.

"I'm sorry," he said finally. "I thought, when you said earlier that you couldn't love somebody like me, that maybe you were just trying to convince yourself you couldn't. I thought maybe you meant that you cared anyway, despite it all." He turned away.

She stumbled toward him. "Dez—don't go!"

And then she was in his arms, and her world had stopped rocking crazily on its axis, tipped to and fro by shock after shock, and it settled once more into equilibrium. The balance was different—and she knew it would be challenging, maybe even risky, to get used to it. But new as it was, it felt right in a way that nothing else in her life ever had.

When Dez stopped kissing her, he laid his cheek against her hair and said huskily, "Another twenty or thirty years of hard work, and you might actually be able to turn me into something besides a barbarian."

"I'll give it a try." She hardly knew what she was saying. "Dez—what did you mean about the things from Essie's house? If we're going to have a condo—"

"On the fifth floor, I think," he mused. "Where they have the hot tubs displayed. That way we can just leave one of them in place and build the condo around it."

"You mean *use* the things from Essie's house in the condo?"

"Some of them—though I was actually thinking further ahead than that. If we take everything we can save from Essie's house, someday we can build a new one and put all those things to use. The stairway, and the light fixtures, and the crown moldings—"

"I didn't realize barbarians knew what a crown molding was."

"You may be surprised at what I know. Anyway, we'll take the best of Essie's house and use it as a framework for our own. The two of us—and our kids."

"Kids?"

"You know. Little people. Rug rats. House apes. Unless you can't stand the thought."

"Of having kids? I've always wanted kids."

"Good." He held her a little away from him, and looked down at her with eyebrows slightly raised. "Though in the interests of honesty I suppose I should confess… You do realize I'm only marrying you so that when our kids want to hear all the stories about Desmond Kerrigan and great-aunt Essie, I can turn them over to you and go play golf.''

She smiled up at him. ''Of course, when you're not around, you won't know what kind of stories I'm telling them. About swinging on kitchen doors, and soaking fig cookies in milk.... Oh, damn.''

''What?''

''The cookie jar. I'd almost forgotten about it.''

''Oh, that. Don't worry about it.'' He leaned in to kiss her once more.

Gina ducked. ''But I can't just—''

''The jar is safe. I gave it to Eleanor to put back in the display, and I came up to your office so I could take you downstairs and show you. Then we got a little distracted.''

''But how—?''

''I was quietly putting the word out to all the pawnshops and fences in town that I'd ransom it. But before I got the chance, the thief got cold feet over what he'd done, and he left it at the television station. You guessed right—he apparently saw the show, and that was what gave him the idea.''

''The guy who came in the day after the show and asked to see it?'' Gina breathed.

''He seems to be the most likely suspect—but we'll probably never know for sure. Carla called me and told me I could have the glory of bringing the jar back to you if I'd give her an exclusive about the tower. Otherwise, she said, she'd bring it herself and take all the credit for recovering it.''

''You didn't give her an interview, surely.''

''Of course I did. I couldn't pass up such a good chance to be your hero. See what you've done to me?'' He kissed her, long and slowly. ''I thought the moment I first saw you that you were trouble.''

"And for once in your life," Gina said, "you were right."

"You know what?" he whispered against her lips. "In this case, I wouldn't have it any other way."

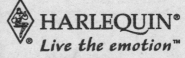

Is your man too good to be true?

Hot, gorgeous AND romantic?
If so, he could be a Harlequin® Blaze™ series cover model!

Our grand-prize winners will receive a trip for two to New York City to
shoot the cover of a Blaze novel, and will stay at the luxurious Plaza Hotel.

Plus, they'll receive $500 U.S. spending money!

The runner-up winners will receive $200 U.S.
to spend on a romantic dinner for two.

It's easy to enter!

In 100 words or less, tell us what makes your boyfriend or spouse a true romantic
and the perfect candidate for the cover of a Blaze novel, and include in your submission
two photos of this potential cover model.

All entries must include the written submission of the contest entrant, two photographs of the model
candidate and the Official Entry Form and Publicity Release forms completed in full and signed by
both the model candidate and the contest entrant. Harlequin, along with the experts at
Elite Model Management, will select a winner.

For photo and complete Contest details, please refer to the Official Rules on the next page. All entries
will become the property of Harlequin Enterprises Ltd. and are not returnable.

**Please visit www.blazecovermodel.com to download a copy of the Official Entry Form and
Publicity Release Form or send a request to one of the addresses below.**

Please mail your entry to: **Harlequin Blaze Cover Model Search**

In U.S.A.	In Canada
P.O. Box 9069	P.O. Box 637
Buffalo, NY	Fort Erie, ON
14269-9069	L2A 5X3

No purchase necessary. Contest open to Canadian and U.S. residents who are 18 and over.
Void where prohibited. Contest closes September 30, 2003.

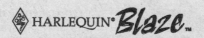

HARLEQUIN BLAZE COVER MODEL SEARCH CONTEST 3569 OFFICIAL RULES
NO PURCHASE NECESSARY TO ENTER

1. To enter, submit two (2) 4" x 6" photographs of a boyfriend or spouse (who must be 18 years of age or older) taken no later than three (3) months from the time of entry: a close-up, waist up, shirtless photograph; and a fully clothed, full-length photograph, then, tell us, in 100 words or fewer, why he should be a Harlequin Blaze cover model and how he is romantic. Your complete "entry" must include: (i) your essay, (ii) the Official Entry Form and Publicity Release Form printed below completed and signed by you (as "Entrant"), (iii) the photographs (with your hand-written name, address and phone number, and your model's name, address and phone number on the back of each photograph), and (iv) the Publicity Release Form and Photograph Representation Form printed below completed and signed by your model (as "Model"), and should be sent via first-class mail to either: Harlequin Blaze Cover Model Search Contest 3569, P.O. Box 9069, Buffalo, NY, 14269-9069, or Harlequin Blaze Cover Model Search Contest 3569, P.O. Box 637, Fort Erie, Ontario L2A 5X3. All submissions must be in English and be received no later than September 30, 2003. Limit: one entry per person, household or organization. **Purchase or acceptance of a product offer does not improve your chances of winning.** All entry requirements must be strictly adhered to for eligibility and to ensure fairness among entries.

2. Ten (10) Finalist submissions (photographs and essays) will be selected by a panel of judges consisting of members of the Harlequin editorial, marketing and public relations staff, as well as a representative from Elite Model Management (Toronto) Inc., based on the following criteria:

Aptness/Appropriateness of submitted photographs for a Harlequin Blaze cover—70%
Originality of Essay—20%
Sincerity of Essay—10%

In the event of a tie, duplicate finalists will be selected. The photographs submitted by finalists will be posted on the Harlequin website no later than November 15, 2003 (at www.blazecovermodel.com), and viewers may vote, in rank order, on their favorite(s) to assist in the panel of judges' final determination of the Grand Prize and Runner-up winning entries based on the above judging criteria. All decisions of the judges are final.

3. All entries become the property of Harlequin Enterprises Ltd. and none will be returned. Any entry may be used for future promotional purposes. Elite Model Management (Toronto) Inc. and/or its partners, subsidiaries and affiliates operating as "Elite Model Management" will have access to all entries including all personal information, and may contact any Entrant and/or Model in its sole discretion for their own business purposes. Harlequin and Elite Model Management (Toronto) Inc. are separate entities with no legal association or partnership whatsoever having no power to bind or obligate the other or create any expressed or implied obligation or responsibility on behalf of the other, such that Harlequin shall not be responsible in any way for any acts or omissions of Elite Model Management (Toronto) Inc. or its partners, subsidiaries and affiliates in connection with the Contest or otherwise and Elite Model Management shall not be responsible in any way for any acts or omissions of Harlequin or its partners, subsidiaries and affiliates in connection with the contest or otherwise.

4. All Entrants and Models must be residents of the U.S. or Canada, be 18 years of age or older, and have no prior criminal convictions. The contest is not open to any Model that is a professional model and/or actor in any capacity at the time of the entry. Contest void wherever prohibited by law; all applicable laws and regulations apply. Any litigation within the Province of Quebec regarding the conduct or organization of a publicity contest may be submitted to the Régie des alcools, des courses et des jeux for a ruling, and any litigation regarding the awarding of a prize may be submitted to the Régie only for the purpose of helping the parties reach a settlement. Employees and immediate family members of Harlequin Enterprises Ltd., D.L. Blair, Inc., Elite Model Management (Toronto) Inc. and their parents, affiliates, subsidiaries and all other agencies, entities and persons connected with the use, marketing or conduct of this Contest are not eligible to enter. Acceptance of any prize offered constitutes permission to use Entrants' and Models' names, essay submissions, photographs or other likenesses for the purposes of advertising, trade, publication and promotion on behalf of Harlequin Enterprises Ltd., its parent, affiliates, subsidiaries, assigns and other authorized entities involved in the judging and promotion of the contest without further compensation to any Entrant or Model, unless prohibited by law.

5. Finalists will be determined no later than October 30, 2003. Prize Winners will be determined no later than January 31, 2004. Grand Prize Winners (consisting of winning Entrant and Model) will be required to sign and return Affidavit of Eligibility/Release of Liability and Model Release forms within thirty (30) days of notification. Non-compliance with this requirement and within the specified time period will result in disqualification and an alternate will be selected. Any prize notification returned as undeliverable will result in the awarding of the prize to an alternate set of winners. All travelers (or parent/legal guardian of a minor) must execute the Affidavit of Eligibility/Release of Liability prior to ticketing and must possess required travel documents (e.g. valid photo ID) where applicable. Travel dates specified by Sponsor but no later than May 30, 2004.

6. Prizes: One (1) Grand Prize—the opportunity for the Model to appear on the cover of a paperback book from the Harlequin Blaze series, and a 3 day/2 night trip for two (Entrant and Model) to New York, NY for the photo shoot of Model which includes round-trip coach air transportation from the commercial airport nearest the winning Entrant's home to New York, NY, (or, in lieu of air transportation, $100 cash payable to Entrant and Model, if the winning Entrant's home is within 250 miles of New York, NY), hotel accommodations (double occupancy) at the Plaza Hotel and $500 cash spending money payable to Entrant and Model, (approximate prize value: $8,000), and one (1) Runner-up Prize of $200 cash payable to Entrant and Model for a romantic dinner for two (approximate prize value: $200). Prizes are valued in U.S. currency. Prizes consist of only those items listed as part of the prize. No substitution of prize(s) permitted by winners. All prizes are awarded jointly to the Entrant and Model of the winning entries, and are not severable - prizes and obligations may not be assigned or transferred. Any change to the Entrant and/or Model of the winning entries will result in disqualification and an alternate will be selected. Taxes on prize are the sole responsibility of winners. Any and all expenses and/or items not specifically described as part of the prize are the sole responsibility of winners. Harlequin Enterprises Ltd. and D.L. Blair, Inc., their parents, affiliates, and subsidiaries are not responsible for errors in printing of Contest entries and/or game pieces. No responsibility is assumed for lost, stolen, late, illegible, incomplete, inaccurate, non-delivered, postage due or misdirected mail or entries. In the event of printing or other errors which may result in unintended prize values or duplication of prizes, all affected game pieces or entries shall be null and void.

7. Winners will be notified by mail. For winners' list (available after March 31, 2004), send a self-addressed, stamped envelope to: Harlequin Blaze Cover Model Search Contest 3569 Winners, P.O. Box 4200, Blair, NE 68009-4200, or refer to the Harlequin website (at www.blazecovermodel.com).

Contest sponsored by Harlequin Enterprises Ltd., P.O. Box 9042, Buffalo, NY 14269-9042.

HDOVOMODEL2

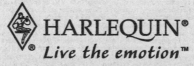

It's romantic comedy with a kick
(in a pair of strappy pink heels)!

Introducing

"It's chick-lit with the romance and happily-ever-after ending that Harlequin is known for."
—*USA TODAY* bestselling author Millie Criswell, author of *Staying Single*, October 2003

"Even though our heroine may take a few false steps while finding her way, she does it with wit and humor."
—Dorien Kelly, author of *Do-Over*, November 2003

Launching October 2003.
Make sure you pick one up!

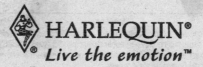

Visit us at www.harlequinflipside.com

HFGENERIC